The Snowflake

JAMIE CARIE

The Snowflake

A Novella

B&H
PUBLISHING GROUP

Nashville, Tennessee

Published by B&H Publishing Group
Nashville, Tennessee

Dewey Decimal Classification: F
Subject Heading: ROMANCES\GOLD MINES AND
MINING—FICTION\ADVENTURE FICTION

Scripture quotations are taken from the Holy Bible,
King James Version. Also quoted: Scripture quotations
marked (NIV) are taken from the Holy Bible, New International
Version®. NIV®. Copyright © 1973, 1978, 1984 by International
Bible Society. Used by permission of Zondervan Publishing
House. All rights reserved.
Carol lyrics for *O Come, O Come, Emmanuel* found in chapter
fourteen can be found at www.carols.org.uk/o_come_come_
emmanuel.htm.

1 2 3 4 5 6 7 8 • 13 12 11 10

To the fathers in my life:

To my father-in-law, Jerry Masopust. If there was a "Biggest Family Fan" award, I would give it to you! Thank you for all the love and support over the years.

To my dad, Jim Carie. You read this one when it was a short story and said it was your favorite. You "get" me like no one else. I think our snowflake patterns must be quite similar.

To my agent, Wes Yoder. Your guidance and care for me is a gift from God for which I am so grateful! This story would not have come to be without you.

And to my heavenly Father. Words cannot express my love for You, though I try with words. Every story, every poem, every song I write is for You.

Acknowledgments

A very special thank-you to my editor, Julee Schwarzburg. It has been such a pleasure working with you and getting to know you. You are all that is warmth and kindness and a brilliant editor besides!

And to the wonder team at B&H: Julie Gwinn, Karen Ball, Haverly Robbe, Kim Stanford, Diana Lawrence, and the sales team. Your love and support for these stories has blessed me more than I can tell you. Thank you from the bottom of my heart!

They say that every snowflake is different. If that
were true, how could the world go on?
How could we ever get up off our knees?
How could we ever recover from the wonder of it?

—Jeanette Winterson, *The Passion*, 1987

Chapter One

Alaska 1897

e there, be there, be there, be there.

The words thudded in time with my heartbeat as I let myself into the cold, tiny cabin aboard the steamship. I turned and shut the door with a soft click. Only a few minutes, that's all I had before my brother would find me missing and come looking for me. Only a few precious minutes alone.

I rushed over the rocking floor to the side of the lower bunk, knelt down, and reached underneath to pull out my heavy trunk. My fingers shook with fright and cold as fumbled with the latch and lifted the lid.

I shoved aside dresses and stockings, a petticoat that had seen better days, and a pair of shabby pink slippers, then dug down to the bottom of the trunk. My fingers crushed around the feel of tulle as tears sprung to my eyes.

It was still there.

My heart lurched, as if it had long forgotten this wave of bliss. My eyelids dropped shut as I lifted out the long veil, stood and clutched it to my chest. I stroked the delicate fabric, unable to look at it yet, savoring the blindness that heightened my touch as my fingertips ran along the silken crown at the top, each faux pearl against the lace a seed of delight. A laughing sob leapt from my throat, and I opened my eyes.

The veil was already two years old. What would happen when I lifted it out and found it yellowed with age?

I'd first seen it in a dressmaker's shop window on a windswept, autumn day in San Francisco. I walked inside that shop without thinking what I was doing.

A woman with gray-and-black streaked hair rushed from a back room, smoothing down her skirts as she stepped into her showroom. She smiled at me, like I could be a paying customer, and I pretended I was.

"How can I help you, my dear?"

I stood mute for a moment and then pointed toward the window. "May I"—I swallowed hard and rushed out the rest before my courage failed completely. "May I see that veil?"

"Of course." The woman turned to fetch it. She was round in a motherly way that made me feel better somehow. "You *must* try it on."

And I did.

I let her arrange the tulle, so long that it flowed from my head to the floor behind me. She fussed over the combs in the headpiece, placing them into my thick crown of curls I was forever trying to manage, trying to conceal their full glory. Rich brown hair as to be almost black, curling all the way down my back but never to be seen—always caught up and away into a hat or cap or knitted net that kept it from any temptation of man. It was understood that I would never let it down.

The woman finished positioning the great white veil on my head, as if it was a normal day's occurrence, and I supposed for her it was. But I'd never had a day like that. She fluffed up the gauzy poof in the back and then gave a great sigh and stood back, her hands over her wide bosom.

"It's perfect." She beamed, gesturing toward a mirror.

I turned toward the wavy glass, my stomach seizing and trembling. As my face came into view, my hand, too, lifted to my chest. I blinked but the image didn't fade; it only grew stronger. Brown, wide-set eyes, round and startled, a thin face, pale against the walnut hue of my hair. The veil was white and stark and beyond beauty. My heart pounded so loud I was sure the woman could hear it. But she only looked at me, over my shoulder in the glass, with a kind smile.

"It's lovely on you, dear. When is your wedding?"

Had the woman spoken? I couldn't hear beyond the roar of my blood. I stared and blinked at my image in the glass. A bride?

Never.

I jerked my gaze away from the glass, unable to see my reflection for another second. My hands clawed at the delicate combs, frantic to free them from my hair.

"Never," I whispered, thrusting the delicate piece into the woman's arms. With tears blinding my eyes, I stumbled from the shop—out into the cold nothingness of my life.

Weeks passed but I couldn't forget. Symbol, talisman, covenant, promise . . . *hope.* It took months of hoarded pennies, lies when questioned about the rise in the cost of flour or milk, and the shattering of my pride to go back to that shop. I knew the woman would look at me with pity in her eyes, but the need to have the veil was greater than any of that. And it was still here in my trunk. Jonah hadn't found it yet.

The door swung open and crashed against the wall.

"Oh!" I turned and faced him, my brother, crushing the veil to my chest. My breath froze as he advanced.

"Where have you been?" His voice was reed thin with a grasping, clawing undertone that I knew only too well.

"I was tired."

"You're up to something. What do you have there?"

He advanced on me. I took a step back and then another until my legs bumped into the room's narrow bench. "It's nothing. Please, I was only going to lie down for a little while."

Panic rose in my throat, suffocating me as his eyes went black. His thin arm struck out like a coiled snake and snatched the delicate tulle.

"No!" I held tight to my precious hope. "Please, it's nothing of value. Let me keep it. Please, I'll do anything."

"A veil." Shock lit his eyes, and then he made a low sound that was so hollow, both terrified and angry—an eerie, mad, moaning sound. "Ellie, you can't leave me. I won't let you leave me."

He tugged harder as his gaze darted around the cabin, as if looking for a place to crawl in and hide. His gaze, suddenly sharp in focus, snapped back to mine. He inhaled. "It's that man, isn't it? You've been talking to him. I saw you."

His grip on the veil tightened as he stepped so close to me our noses nearly touched and his breath came and went in quick gasps across my face.

"There is no man, Jonah. Please, it's just a memento. It was mother's. I keep it to remember her by." The lies flowed easy and vivid, but I could tell by the trembling of his lips and the rage eating up his eyes that he did not believe me.

He grasped my wrists in a searing hold. His hands, so seemingly frail and weak, were stronger than a steel trap. The cloth of the veil twisted around my hands and his. With one hand holding one of my wrists against the wall, he jerked my other hand up and out.

I cried out in pain as the veil made a long ripping sound. My eyes clenched shut as sobs escaped my usually tight throat. *"No."* I turned my face away from him toward the wall and wailed.

Loud footsteps rang across the floor, and then Jonah was wrenched away from me. My eyes blinked open, pools of heartbreak rolling down my cheeks as the man of my dreams held my brother's arms behind his back.

I watched, unable to utter a word, as he hissed into Jonah's ear. "What is the meaning of this? If you ever lay a hand on her again—"

He didn't finish the threat, but Jonah's eyes went blank, dead. He looked like a little boy again. The boy I'd always protected.

"Don't hurt him."

Buck Lewis shook his head at me. "No one deserves to live like this."

"I'm all he has." My voice was a whisper. Everything in the room went deadly quiet as Buck studied my shattered, pleading eyes.

An enormous crash interrupted my horror. The ship lurched and tilted as a great splintering, the groaning and cracking of ice, exploded in sound. I fell back against the wall as Jonah used the moment of distraction to slither away from Buck's hold.

"Come on!" Buck turned toward the opening in the doorway. "The ship may be damaged. We can't stay down here."

The three of us rushed to the top deck.

It was true. The steamer was locked in ice, inescapably gripped in the cold fingers of winter. I looked around at the collapsed faces, mirroring misery, the tall and lanky down to the short and stocky, all on the verge of a full-blown panic.

I wanted to say, "I told you so," to try and tell Jonah in a hundred different pleading ways before this God-forsaken journey began, but knowing better, knowing it wouldn't change the next time he got that stubborn, tight-lipped look. I kept my mouth closed. Silly men. Silly dreaming baby-men. Always wanting to conquer, to kill, and then build it up all over again. A tiny laugh bubbled up into my throat as I studied them from the edge of the crowd—hating them, loving them, scoffing and admiring.

Captain Henry Conrad stood at the bow of the steamer looking smaller than his six feet and 250 pounds, diminished by the simple law that in certain conditions water turns to ice. He gestured at the crumpled map in his hand while the moaning wind whipped red into our cheeks. The men crowded around him, knowing the truth but wanting to hear it explained. Their dreams of riches, for the duration of this Alaskan winter at least, were over.

Sinclair, a man who wore his father's idealism on a chubby-cheeked face, cursed a violent streak. "That Yankee in Seattle promised we'd make it. I knew we shouldn't take a Yankee's word for it." He slung his hands into the pockets of a pair of expensive trousers, causing the seam to strain against his backside, and scowled at the broad, whiskered face of the captain.

"It ain't anybody's fault the Yukon River freezes up so early," put in the tall, lanky Zeke Robbins. "We were straddling the seasons, pushing as far and as fast as we could, and we knew it." Zeke only needed a stalk of wheat to chew on and a floppy hat to complete the picture of the middle-American farmer.

"We may as well face it, gents." The captain intervened before a full-fledged fight could break out. "We'll be sitting out the winter right here, huddled together on this pile of wood, unable to move an inch until spring thaw."

What would that mean to the lone woman of the expedition? Should I be afraid? Would my brother protect me?

Or would he only accuse me of self-absorbed romanticism should I voice any hint of my scandalous concern?

Several voices cried out in stubborn rebellion to the idea of giving up until the clean voice of another quieted them. "As I see it, gentlemen, we have one other choice."

They turned in eager silence, necks craning, bodies leaning in, straining for a way out of the certain despair that would engulf them at the end of this meeting. If any man could salvage this mess, it was Buck Lewis, and they all knew it. They'd heard such in bits and pieces of stories that made him out a hero and a legend.

I studied him. What was it about him that held me so entranced? He had a weathered face, bold with a hint of recklessness, intelligent blue eyes that could cause a lesser man to turn away, a lean-muscled body with reflexes that could save a life, and an easy common sense that made him the voice of reason in turbulent times. The young men idolized him. The older men respected him.

I had tried, for the first few weeks of this journey anyway, to ignore him.

It wasn't that I couldn't feel his presence the moment he neared or didn't feel as if I knew him every time our gazes locked. Oh no. Everything in me wanted to follow that pantherlike stride as he walked by—with my eyes and my feet and then reach toward him with my hands and my lips. And then he'd spoken to me and all was lost.

Buck stared each man in the eye. "You should know what you're in for. If you plan to stay, you'll be looking into the face of starvation, hoping it doesn't look back. Hunting parties will go out daily with the threat of sudden blizzards and wild animals to hound your heels. When the food runs out, the unfathomable will start looking pretty. It may come down to the strong surviving, but the means of that survival might not be something you can go to bed with. Might be something you have to wrestle over for the remainder of your days."

He paused, scanning their collective gaze, taking stock. "For those who don't like the sound of that and still want to reach Dawson City before spring, they can trust in dogs and sleds and pray for enough good weather to mush overland."

"What are you going to do, Buck?"

"How many miles to Dawson?"

"When will the food run out?"

Buck answered the first question. "I'll be going to Dawson." He paused, then continued with a flat slap to his voice. "It won't be an easy trip. It's a good two hundred miles. That's a week's worth of walking in bitter temperatures with the food running out."

"But we'd make it, right, Buck?" A freckle-faced young man from Iowa squinted up at him. Buck could have said the sky was made of cotton candy and this boy would have nodded in agreement.

Buck gave him a hard look. "I don't know, but you are welcome to join me and see."

A grim contemplation fell on them as each considered the odds.

Sinclair was the first to speak. "I didn't come this far to cool my heels all winter on this ice barge. I'm coming with you."

Buck nodded, but his eyes said he would rather take a marauding grizzly along. Ronnie Nelson, George

McCallister, Adam Walker, and Randy Olsen volunteered, all young and strong and capable.

"I'll be going with you."

My head jerked up as my gaze swung toward the familiar voice. Why would my ragged, haunted brother want to take on something so dangerous?

Buck matched my reaction. "What about your sister? You would leave her on board?"

Jonah scowled. "She'll be coming with us."

Buck's gaze found mine on the other side of the crowd, hugging the outskirts. Why did he care when no one ever had? I wasn't worthy of attention from a man like Buck Lewis, and it was only a matter of time until he figured that out.

Buck turned back to Jonah. "You explain to her how rough it will be, or I will. Then, if she's determined, well then, she'll know."

My brother's face turned stony at the rapid-fire orders, but he nodded. He wouldn't tell me anything of the sort, but Buck wouldn't know that I would have already thought out every detail, every possibility for success or failure, and planned for it the best I could.

It was my job to take care of Jonah, not the other way around.

As the men scattered into disheartened, muttering groups, Buck watched Jonah grip Ellen's arm and pull her back toward their cabin. A feeling of fierce protectiveness rose so strong that his muscles leapt to follow them, but he clamped down the urge with gritted teeth and a clinched fist around the rail as a tether. He was on a mission, and Ellen Pierce was not part of the plan. He needed to remember that.

He turned toward the ice-clogged water and squeezed his eyes shut, but the vision of her was even stronger in the dark. He remembered the first moment he'd seen her on the steamer. She'd been just across the deck, not more than ten feet, then she turned around and looked up at him. She was the kind of woman that stole a man's breath at first, taking a moment for the shock to wear off and his jumped heart to settle down. But he could have grown used to that. He could have resisted the ethereal depths of her dark eyes that spoke pain and passion in equal measure, but then he went and did a fool thing: He spoke to her.

"You're not traveling alone, are you?" It had been a stupid thing to say.

She gave him a quick smile, a gentle curve of rose-colored lips, and a flash of fearful reticence in her eyes before looking down and then behind her. "No, my brother is with me."

She was as skittish as a new colt, but she didn't run away. She stood there, eyes downcast, waiting for him to say something else.

His mind went blank and his mouth went dry. What was wrong with him? He was never this unsure of himself. "You got a name?" Had he really just asked her that? Of course she had a name. A warm flush filled his cheeks and he looked away.

She didn't seem to notice. She took a step forward and held out a mittened hand. "Ellen Pierce, and you?" She smiled, with just a hint of a teasing light in her eyes. "Do you have a name?"

Buck cleared his throat and reached for her hand. It was small but the grip was comfortable, like two puzzle pieces locking together. "Buck Lewis. Pleased to meet you, ma'am."

Ellen gazed up at him through thick, dark lashes, and his heart did a double beat. His wife, whom he had loved more than life itself, had never made him feel like this . . . this floating, dizzy, anchorless unease.

Before he could say something else that would make him look like an idiot, a man strode over with angry, clipped steps, came up from behind her, and grasped her arm, wrenching her hand out of his. He glared at Buck. "Is this man bothering you, Ellie?"

Ellen backed away shaking her head. "He just introduced himself, Jonah. Please don't make a scene." She whispered the last in a terse tone.

"You stay away from my sister, got it?"

So this was her brother. A small, wiry man with sunken cheeks and eyes. Physically he presented no threat, but those eyes. . . . A strange darkness possessed them that sent a shiver down Buck's spine.

"I didn't mean any harm." Buck spoke in a low, calm voice as he would to a cornered animal.

"Just stay away from her." Her brother pulled her away with a jerk on her arm.

Buck curled his hand into a fist. That had been the first of many times he saw Jonah manhandling her, and every time Buck wanted to plow his fist into the gaunt face. He kicked at the side of the ship as he thought back to what he witnessed today.

Her brother was growing more dangerous, demented even. What if he snapped? Killed her? Buck didn't want to care, shouldn't care, but he did. *Lord, what can I do about it?*

His wife's face, her eyes, how they'd widened with the shock of the bullet as it entered her chest, flashed before him and nearly sent him to his knees. He hadn't been able to protect her. He had insisted she come with him to Skagway. Kalage's death was his fault.

God, why didn't You stop me? Why didn't You stop him?

Buck quieted his mind and tried to hear God's answer. He closed his eyes and waited.

Nothing.

He heard nothing but the deadness of his laden heart and the moaning of ice all around.

The early morning air had a stinging crispness that felt different somehow, as if we were inhaling crystallized snowflakes into our lungs instead of air. Garbed in my tattered coat and mittens, I followed the fourteen men setting out for Klondike gold and the city in the north that made poor men's dreams come true: Dawson City. Our only assets were three heavily loaded sleds with motley beasts for dogs and inexperienced mushers for drivers.

I looked at the facts around me and tried to do what Buck told us to do—pray the clear skies would hold—but I choked on the first line. I didn't pray anymore, hadn't prayed in years.

What could my brother be thinking to command that we do this? I'd tried to convince him the night before. The memory of him curling into a ball on the bed and rocking back and forth with low moaning swept through me.

I went to him, tried to comfort him with a hand on his back. "Jonah, we would be safer waiting out the winter here on the steamer. Please. You're not thinking clearly."

He turned, snarled, and then spit at me. Before the shock of that wore off, he leaned into my face and, with a guttural sound to his voice, let loose a stream of curse words, evil horrid words directed at me, about me. His face contorted with a hatred I'd not seen before. I backed away from his crazed eyes, but he grabbed me.

"I will tether you to a dogsled if necessary. I'm going to get me a claim, and even if it kills you, Ellie, you are going with me." His eyes rolled back in his head. He began to shake and sob. "Don't leave me alone, Ellie. Don't do it."

I saw it then. That dark presence that haunted him, a specter I could neither see nor hear but recognized the signs of all too well. It grew stronger, desperate, at times like these. Sometimes it had us running like rabbits, moving from city to city. Sometimes it watched us hide in Jonah's make-believe world, where he was god and king and could do anything. And then there were the times it just hovered in a low hum, coloring his every thought and action and eating away at his flesh until I could hardly remember the strong, handsome youth I had known as my brother so many years ago.

Despair filled me as my cage, that promise I'd made to my mother, clamped around me. "Yes, I'll go, Jonah. Don't cry."

He abruptly let go of my wrist and collapsed on the bed like a limp rag doll. I spent the rest of the night quietly packing our things.

Now I fumbled with the straps of the snowshoes that would supposedly allow me to skate across the depths of white. Buck walked among us, checking the packs, explaining the duties, the protocol that was our only chance of walking upright into Dawson.

Most nodded their sober understanding, a few ventured questions, but Sinclair puffed out his chest and flat out complained when told he would walk instead of drive a sled.

"I don't know who you think you are, Lewis, and who made you leader, but I'm not taking orders from the likes of you."

Buck pinned him with a steely glare and stated loud enough for all to hear, "Some trail advice, Sinclair. Plan on taking the worst of the chores, the lowliest of positions for the next week. And then, if you get better, consider yourself lucky. We work together to stay alive." He turned his back on the seething man, giving me my first real shudder of the horror that lay ahead.

Men like that could ruin us.

When Buck came to me, he paused, his first hesitation of the morning. He waited for me to stare back into his ice blue eyes, reminding me of the floating crystal in the air, as breath robbing . . . and as cold. "You sure about this, Miss Pierce?"

He wanted to hear it from my lips. He needed to hear me say it. I also knew that if I said I did not wish to go, he would overpower my brother's demand and see that I stayed the winter on board the steamer.

The trail ahead would be harder than anything I'd known, miles of wading through the cold, deep tundra, but the ship behind me was full of men I didn't know or trust. With Buck and my brother gone, it would only be a matter of time before they found plausible reason to abuse me, but I might have a better chance of living through that.

I hesitated, feeling the tension in Jonah's body beside me, seeing the hidden hope in the man's eyes before me. "I'll go."

Buck nodded and turned away, but not before I saw the tanned skin around his eyes crinkle, a fine web of lines from some long-forgotten place of happiness, and then I heard his deep exhale.

Chapter Two

The dark line of prodding figures stretched out against a field of white. Buck looked back for what seemed like the hundredth time that hour. The weaker members had dropped back, their panting breaths telling in the fixed puffs of fog that created ice on beards and mustaches and eyebrows. This wasn't good, not good at all.

He waved his hands above his head and shouted at them. "Keep up! Stay together!" He had to push them harder, knowing their strength would only ebb over the next unmerciful days. Praise God, Ellen was doing all right, even helping her brother when he floundered in a drift.

Pride swelled his heart every time he looked at her. She was so . . . strong and steady, calm and helpful, seeing a need and meeting it the best she could. But their group had its weak members too. By nightfall two men had decided to return to the steamboat and pray for a short winter.

As dusk settled on the land, Buck motioned for the group to gather around. "We'll stop and camp for the night. Ronnie, you and George gather what firewood and branches you can find so we can thaw our food and feet."

Buck let a crack of a smile come through, trying for encouragement. They all looked at him with white, wide-eyed faces, and Buck knew they were feeling the fear, some bordering on panic. It was only the first day, but most of them had never experienced such cold.

"What can I do?"

He turned to see Ellen close by his side. It never failed to give his heart a start when she was that close to him, and he wasn't sure why. Sure, she was one of the prettiest women he'd ever seen, but he had never been attracted to exceptionally pretty women. They were usually too doll-like and prissy for his taste. And Ellen was doll-like in the sense that her face had perfect proportions, her form was thin and willowy, but that's where the comparison ended. She was a contradiction that fascinated him. Where she should be weak, she proved strong; and where she could be needy or flirtatious or, well, fake, she wasn't ever any of those things.

"You can help me pass out dinner." He led her over to the sled that held the food. Her brother glared at him, but he ignored it. It would be a miracle if the man had the strength to glare at anyone for much longer.

After the simple meal, the group sank on the green spruce boughs two of the men had cut and spread around the fire for beds. Ellen lay a few feet away, close enough he could see she was shivering. He wanted to take her into his arms and hold her against the warmth of his chest, but that would cause too much trouble with the other men, and one man in particular. If he upset Jonah's delicate mental balance, Buck knew who would suffer.

He looked over the camp one last time before lying down. The dogs had had their dinner—frozen salmon, whacked off with an ax and wolfed down before the men could turn their backs on them—and were huddled in heaps, licking snow from between the pads in their feet before succumbing to sleep in their curling cocoons.

Each man had been assigned his chores: cooking, hunting, setting up and breaking down camp, or taking care of the dogs. None of them liked it after a harrowing day on the trail when the flesh demanded the ease of being parallel to the earth, but they'd done it uncomplaining, except for the muttered curses of Sinclair. Buck's eyes narrowed as he stared at the big man's back.

Sinclair.

There was a man to watch.

It was the third day when I first noticed it. Jonah was slowing. His breath was more labored, more ragged after just two hours on the trail. His steps faltered beside me, but when I glanced in concern, he scowled at me. Clearly I was not to notice.

I dared not comment. He would store and nurse any injury to his pride and repay me later when he was able, with weeks of belittling, soul-smothering attacks. Instead, I pretended I didn't know we were falling behind, pretended it was normal to invent reasons for running ahead to see the dark coat of the last man and so to discover our way. It was a game I had become an expert at—this make-believe world where Jonah's mind and soul were safe.

We arrived at camp nearly an hour after the rest, by now so frozen my muscles quivered with fatigue as I helped my brother limp to his snowy bed. Buck's gaze followed us in a worried way, his brows raised at me in question. I nodded to him, assuring him we would be all right when I didn't believe anything of the sort. I would have to approach Buck, find out how we were going to go on tomorrow, but first I had my evening chores and Jonah's too. He would be unable to rise now that he had his boots off, his gaze fixed on his feet, which looked as hard and frail as porcelain.

We all moved like a clock needing to be wound, our blood thick in its efforts to bring any life to our limbs. My mind too was affected. I couldn't think, couldn't concentrate on mixing the flour for our evening biscuits. Had I added enough water? I couldn't tell by the thick paste I stirred, my fingers locked with cold around the handle of the spoon.

A hand on my shoulder startled me, causing me to turn sharply and stumble. Buck caught me, righted me, lingering, touching, still strong somehow, still everything they said he was.

"I'm sorry." I pulled away.

"Miss Pierce, how are you? Really."

Really? This man wanted the truth? Shock and something else, something that felt close to relief, spread through my limbs, making them weak and alive at the same time.

"Call me Ellen." My lips curled up into the unfamiliar gesture of a smile. Had Jonah seen it? He would not like me talking to Buck, much less smiling at him.

Turning as brisk as my muddled mind allowed, I stated, "I'm cold, Mr. Lewis, but I find I can walk well enough."

I paused, afraid but needing the help. "My brother will not come to you, but I fear his feet are in jeopardy. His toes are black on the ends. Do you know how to save them?"

Buck took a breath, his gaze sliding toward Jonah, and nodded. "I thought as much. What kind of footgear is he wearing, Ellen?"

He said it . . . used my name like he was savoring the feel of it on his tongue. "Boots, leather boots." I looked down at Buck's brown knee-high moccasins.

He answered my unspoken question. "Moccasins are waterproof. What are you wearing?"

I lifted the hem of my skirt enough to reveal sturdy leather boots, much like my brother's.

"I have an extra pair of moccasins in my pack you can have. They should fit you. I'm sorry I don't have anything to offer your brother. Whenever we break camp, he needs to put his feet in front of the fire and set his socks and boots up close to dry. Being wet is the enemy in this land. It can take a healthy man down in a few hours. Make him change socks often, even if he has to stop to do it. If his feet aren't frozen, he'll catch up."

I nodded compliance to the rapid-fire instructions as he walked over to his pack, rummaged through it, and came back with some long, folded-over caribou hide. The way he held it, close to him, his thumb caressing a string of beads that adorned the side told me they meant something to him.

An intense wave of jealousy spiked through me and then, the moment I recognized it, dismay. I couldn't take something so precious to him. And yet they might mean the difference between continuing or stopping in another day or two. I thought of Jonah's toes, the pain and suffering of walking on such feet. I reached for the moccasins held from Buck's strong hands.

"Thank you." I turned away, not wanting to see what it cost him to give them to me.

"Don't you want to know?"

I faced him, blinking the water back into the wells of my eyes. "Yes . . . no . . . do you want to tell me? You don't have to tell me."

"They were my wife's, a Tlingit woman." He took a few steps toward me, blocking me from the view of the camp.

"Were?"

"She was shot during a skirmish in the streets of Skagway over an ounce of gold." Buck leaned to one side and tried to spit, his voice hard, his mouth a bitter twist, but it turned to ice barely inches from his lips and crackled into the snow. "This is a God-forsaken place, Ellen, it surely is."

"I thought you loved it here."

"I guess I did at one time, before this gold rush changed everything. Greed taints the land now." A sudden noise sounded from across the camp. The hunters. And they were empty-handed.

Buck's voice was low, for my ears alone. "We'll have to ration in earnest without fresh meat. It will weaken everyone, and a few, like your brother, already have the dead flesh creeping up on the living." He looked into my eyes. "I can't tell this to the others. They wouldn't know what to do with it, but you need to know the truth. Prepare your-self, Ellen. This march is about to turn ugly."

The fourth day one of the dogs dropped and wouldn't get up. Those close enough watched in silence as Buck cut her out of her traces and then, without a word, steered the rest of the panting, stricken animals around her. We passed her body, one by one, trying to avoid the pained, alert eyes, all of us wondering . . . who would be next?

By noon the feeling of warmth was a hazy, rose-colored memory. It was easy to forget why we were doing this. Why had I let Jonah drag me across a continent in search of a pot of gold? There were no rainbows on my horizon. No, I corrected through the stupor of my brain, he had insisted I come along. And when I'd said I wouldn't go . . .

I shivered with the memory of his hands around my throat, the black frenzy in his eyes, the strength he sud-denly possessed. That was the first time I thought he might really be capable of killing me. The time I finally admitted to myself that his violent episodes were escalating in intensity so I was truly no longer safe with him. But what could I do? He would not survive without me, and besides, I had promised my mother to take care of him until the very end.

I looked up from the blinding snow to see that everyone had slowed. Even though my brother and I brought up the rear, it was easy to see the weaving, tottering, drunken-like figures in front of us and know the way.

Jonah leaned more heavily against my side, making my muscles quiver and spasm. I glanced at his face, ice crusting over his nose and chin, bright red spots of color on his cheeks. His breath labored and steps faltered, but I did my best to drag his skeletal form along.

By late afternoon we were stopping often so I could support Jonah while racking coughs consumed his body. It was the ailment Buck had warned about. When the air became so cold it froze in the lungs, the result was a lifetime of coughing for those lucky enough to escape death.

We set up camp later than usual that night and were all as sleepwalkers in our chores. One of the sleds held the food for the group, only to be touched by Buck, whose responsibility it was to dole out the rations for dinner each evening.

I watched him surreptitiously in a degree of safety since Jonah was propped up near the fire, grimacing with the pain of thawing feet. Buck's movements held me entranced: the controlled, supple grace of wilderness-honed muscle; his moccasins clinging to his calves; the fringe and subtle beading of his jacket that a lesser man would look foolish in; the chest and shoulders that fell back, erect and sure . . . the face of a man who knew himself, who spoke his pain out loud, his every word sounding like *truth*.

My heart thudded in my chest, louder and stronger than it had through all the travails of snowbound marching. God help me, I had to get a hold of myself. Jonah would never let me go, and besides, a man like Buck wouldn't want me.

But I couldn't look away. He peeled back the frozen tarpaulin to inventory the food as he did every night. His face became tense, his movements swift and economical and . . . angry. Something was wrong. I could sense it in the way he rechecked his work. Buck never wasted precious energy. Something had to be wrong.

I found myself walking toward him. I didn't stop until I was close enough to see his breath, a cloud of vapor in the frosty air. I breathed it in, shameless in wanting the only part of him I could have. "Buck," my voice faltered, and I wondered if I really wanted to hear the answer, "what is it?"

He froze, staring at me, the connection palpable. "The beef is missing and some of the flour too. We won't make it without that food."

Forever ruthlessly honest.

I didn't quite know how to reconcile it, this constant truth facing after a life built on lies to keep Mother and Jonah feeling safe, but Buck continued. "There is enough for each of us to have a couple of biscuits. If the hunting party doesn't come back with some meat soon, the weakness will overcome us all."

It was strange being someone's helpmate, someone's confidant. I had always held my own council and made decisions for my family the best I could, working with and around Mother and Jonah's inabilities for a normal life. What would it be like to share thoughts and feelings, to come to conclusions together? I could barely imagine the comfort of it, to have someone to hold life's reins with me. Someone who loved me and cared what happened to me as I him. The thought took my breath away.

Buck handed me the remaining flour. "Make up some bread with this, two small biscuits per person. Give them one tonight and we'll save the other for tomorrow at noon. I'll handle the rest. Don't say a word."

"How did this happen? Who did it?"

"I have a good idea." Buck nodded toward a man. "Who among us lacks the pinched-faced, weak limbs of near starvation? I see only one man who has enough energy left over to glare at me at the end of the day. I know of only one man who could convince himself that he has more reason to live than the rest of us."

I looked to where his words led. Sinclair. Of course.

As the biscuits were passed out, Buck stared back into the questioning, gaunt faces with stoic briskness. "We're cutting back. Have to make it last in case we don't get fresh meat."

Buck waited until everyone was bedded down and asleep before making his move. He was responsible for the well-being of the members of this trek, and he wasn't about to let one man ruin them. Sinclair didn't know who he was dealing with if he thought Buck would let him get away with the stolen food.

He eased from his bedroll, then stood, breathing in the bitter air, reaching for the cold handle of his pistol. He crept over to the sleeping form. Sinclair was using his pack as a pillow, but Buck was ready. He aimed the pistol at Sinclair's nose and slid the heavy canvas out from under the man's head.

Sinclair woke with a start, rose to the click of the gun being cocked, and then jerked back as it was rammed between his eyes.

"Whaaattt?"

"Don't move a muscle."

Buck pressed the gun hard against the big man's fore-head and, with his other hand, dumped out the contents of the bag. He pawed through the articles, mixing them with snow. He couldn't believe it. No sign of the stolen food.

Turning on the man, he bit out, "I know you stole the food, Sinclair. Listen carefully. If a single man dies on this trail due to starvation, you will pay in kind. Do you understand? You had better sit up the night and pray God's blessing on the health of this group, or so help me, I will kill you now."

He wouldn't really kill the man, of course, but the threat seemed to work as Sinclair's eyes widened and his face went white. "I didn't steal anything. I'm as hungry as the rest of you."

Buck stared at him long and hard. "You a praying man, Sinclair? 'Cause I thought I just told you to get to your knees." Buck held the gun on the man and waited.

Sinclair scrambled up, clasped his hands together, and closed his eyes in apparent obedience. That should keep him busy for a while.

Buck backed away toward his bedroll. He glanced around at the sleeping forms, his gaze settling on Ellen. *Lord, we need fresh meat or to find that food. I couldn't bear it if I let another woman under my care die.*

The morning brought a heavy snow, the kind that covered us like a fluffy, deadly blanket. I rose from the suffocation in a jerking movement of arms flailing, lungs taking gulping breaths, my hands brushing the snow from my nose and mouth in a panic. I counted the other rising forms, seeing Jonah turn and struggle beside me.

That day the snow was deeper than ever before. I watched Jonah as we stumbled through it, the hair of his beard poking out in stark contrast to his ashen skin, his breath ragged, his eyes as black as death. We both knew it, but I dared not say anything. Jonah might yet have the strength to command the pretend world.

A laugh of hysteria bubbled from my throat. My frozen fingers pressed against my mouth, trying to suppress it, but

I couldn't. There was no use pretending anymore. I leaned away from him and stared into his empty eyes.

"You're dying," I said in a soft and sudden rush. I reached out to touch his face, trying to remember the little boy I had played with as a child.

His black eyes found mine, his pupils so dilated the darkness took over the brown irises. It was as if he weren't there anymore, as if someone else was.

Fear washed over me in a thousand prickles. I moved away from him, staggering but upright. I could still feel my feet.

He stumbled. He fell, flailing in the snow, like a drowning man. I watched . . . horrified and hopeful . . . hating myself . . . and holding my breath. Fate had finally stepped in. I was about to be free.

He landed facedown, unable to turn over. I could save him. I could walk over, shove his shoulder, and give air to his lungs, but what was the point? I couldn't carry him any longer.

If I was going to survive, I would have to sever the anchor and move on, as light and free as a snowflake on the wind.

His sudden rally sent a shock of fresh fear through me. I stilled and stared as he rose out of the great white and plowed toward me.

I ran. Feeling his breath on my neck, I stumbled through the knee-deep snow.

His panting was loud, heavy, and hard on my heels, catching me, throwing his weight onto my back, making me fall face-first into the bitter cold.

I struggled, trying to outmaneuver him, knowing that even in his weakened state, some evil force strengthened him enough to smother me for my moment's betrayal. I'd never done that before—chosen my need before his. He would kill me for it.

We wrestled in snowflakes: cold, heavy, lung-filling, air-robbing beauty. A man, with a man's desperation and a woman with a woman's hope and a force of nature that could bury us beneath it all. We wrestled in snowflakes.

Chapter Three

I stumbled into camp, my only company the wind that sought out my exposed skin and took my breath with it as it rose, singing, back up into the snow-covered mountains surrounding us. I knew Buck had been watching for me by the way his shoulders relaxed when he saw me.

"Where's Jonah?"

"I left him."

Did I say it with joy? How many times I'd envisioned those words, the circumstances that might cause them, the people I would say them to. I didn't know he would be dead when I said it.

"You left him." Buck stared long into my eyes.

I swayed with exhaustion and elation and all of the wretched, glorious truth of it. The words tumbled out like a long-stopped fountain. "He fell. I cut him out of the traces, like you do with the dogs when they fall and . . . and I left him there."

He gripped my face between hard, warm hands, strong and knowing hands. "Is he alive?"

I shook my head, knowing the look in my eyes was as wild as I felt. "He's dead. My brother is dead."

"You are sure? We could send out a search party . . ." He left the words hanging, both of us knowing that no one had the strength to go back. It would be a miracle if we could continue to go forward.

I shook my head, tears of freeing rain rolling down my cheeks. "I should have dragged his body here so he could have a decent burial. I should have—"

Buck shook my shoulders, his gaze piercing like blue lightning. "Ellen, listen to me. He was dying. We all saw it.

It was only a matter of time." He squeezed my shoulders in a tender-tight grip. "You couldn't have dragged him and you know it. You did the only thing you could."

I shuddered, shaking from head to toe, nodding at the truth of his words while my eyes overflowed with tears that instantly froze on my cheeks.

"Okay then." He took me into his arms where it was warm and safe. His shoulder felt just as I had imagined it would.

After a long while Buck led me to the fire and pressed both Jonah's and my last biscuit into my chest. "Keep up your strength; he would want you to have it. God knows I would have done anything to save my wife." He added the last in low bitterness as he raised the bread to my mouth.

I chewed the frozen morsel out of duty, my gaze locked to his, knowing Jonah would have wanted me to choke on it.

The snow again covered us while we slept, blowing bits of dancing elegance and deadly ice. The freckle-faced farm boy, the youngest among us, and two dogs didn't rise in the morning. As we stood in a circle around their snow grave and said a prayer, exhaustion made me too wrung out to even cry.

Buck's prayer sounded like everything he did—sure, confident, that balance of humility mixed with a bone-deep, trusting faith that rang with the knowledge of who he was as a man and where he stood as a creation of God.

I'd never known either.

I laid a wreath of leafy, frozen stems, their leaves slick and solid with ice, upon the mound that would serve as a grave, and then we all turned and packed up for another day of laborious marching.

"Buck, how long ago did your wife die?" The question escaped my vocal chords even though I knew I shouldn't be talking. It was wasteful and greedy to ask him questions when we should reserve each heartbeat for the test ahead.

He glanced over at me, met my eyes, and seemed to be weighing whether to start this conversation. "Last spring, about seven months ago."

"Were you married long?"

Buck gazed straight ahead, but I saw the infinitesimal nod. "Going on five years."

I was quiet, thinking about that. My parents were married about the same amount of time before . . . before my father left. I was three and Jonah five. I had little flickers of memories of my father—the feel of his beard against my cheek, being lifted into the air and shrieking with terrified delight as he spun with me above his head, my mother's face when he left for work one day and did not come back. The look on her face a month later, a year later, and at the end of her life. Her eyes had gone from pain-filled questioning to lifeless stone.

"You never married?" Buck's question interrupted my memories.

I shook my head in a quick movement. At twenty-four I supposed I was an old maid. "With her last breath my mother made me promise to take care of Jonah. He didn't like it if a man started showing interest in me. We moved twice to different cities when a man seemed determined enough to begin courting."

"You had to take care of your brother? Shouldn't it have been the other way around?"

I tapped my forehead with my finger. "Jonah wasn't quite right after my father left us. Something snapped inside him. I didn't know what to do, how to help him, and by the time my mother died, he couldn't hold a job for very long. He wouldn't eat or bathe. He always thought people were watching or following us. He especially didn't like it if a man showed any interest in me."

"So, you've never been in love?"

I laughed and it sounded more bitter than I liked. "Never even been kissed."

Buck stopped, his gaze locked with mine and then dropped to my lips as a gradual thoughtfulness spread across his face.

I blushed and dropped my gaze, more out of breath than the marching was causing.

He reached out and took my snowy, mittened hand in his, his look of calm assurance telling me he didn't care that the men behind us would notice and speculate. "I reckon that will change someday."

He sounded bemused instead of the sadness that thickened his tone when he spoke of his wife. I wasn't sure if he thought he would correct my lack of experience or someone else, now that my warden was gone. A part of me hoped he was referring to himself, but another part of me knew his heart still belonged to another. I pulled my hand from his grip, and we started walking again.

"What was your wife's name?"

"Kalage was her Tlingit name, but the English name she went by was Deborah."

"Which name did you call her?"

Buck flushed, looking embarrassed for the first time.

I raised my brows at him. "You can tell me."

Buck turned his head and mumbled something. "It sounds silly." He sped up our pace through the knee-deep snow.

"I won't think it's silly."

"I called her my Little Two-Face because she was so quiet and shy in front of others and so stubborn and sure of herself when it was just the two of us." He chuckled. "Once she smacked me over the head with a frying pan, and no one would believe it of her when I told my friends why I had a lump the size of a goose egg on my head."

"A frying pan?" I widened my eyes at him and laughed. "What had you done?"

Buck shrugged and then cast a glance toward me with a glimmer of humor in his eyes. "I only said I didn't like her cooking. She made these horrible-tasting Tlingit meals, and one day I had choked down the last one. I told her to learn how to cook like a regular American woman."

A laugh escaped my throat. I would have liked her. "And did she? Learn to cook like you wanted?"

Buck sobered. "She didn't have time. Though I think she would have. She was shot a couple of weeks later."

"I'm sorry, Buck."

"Yeah. Me too."

"Is that why you are going to Dawson City? Are you tracking them?"

Buck studied me for a moment, assessment in his eyes. "I can't go on with my life until I confront her killer. I need to know how any . . . person . . ."—he struggled to continue—"could be so careless, so"—his fists balled up and his throat worked—"heinous as to shoot someone and then run off." His voice lowered to rough rasping, and his eyes filled with tears as he stared into my eyes. "Maybe I'll be careless. Maybe my gun will slip as I'm forcing the story out of him and hauling him to the Northwest Mounted Police office. Maybe so."

His words made me shiver. It felt colder now, the air sweeping in and stinging the exposed skin of my neck. The gray sky above me held nothing but more emptiness.

It was the sixth day of the snowbound march. Just one, maybe two more days, and they should reach Dawson City. Buck took out his compass and watched the needle shiver as if it were freezing, then point northeast.

He took shallow breaths, noting that the temperature was dropping. Any deep breaths brought spasms to his lungs. *Lord, this isn't good. It isn't good at all. No food and the temperature dropping. We need fresh meat and a warm breeze, Lord. And we're going to need both soon.*

Buck turned toward the group, all readying for the day's march, and scanned the men, assessing their strength. They were all moving in a slow-motion daze, but he called over the strongest three.

"I'm sending the three of you to scout for fresh meat." He looked each one, direct and hard, in the eye. "I don't need to tell you how badly we need this, and I'm depending on each of you to stay strong and do your best."

They nodded somber agreement.

"Fan out and continue northeast so you don't fall too far behind the rest of us."

"Someone needs to question Sinclair, boss. We all know he did it." Ronnie Nelson forced the words between clenched teeth.

Buck nodded. Word had spread that someone had stolen provisions, and suspicious eyes hardened by the restless desperation of hunger followed the one man they all thought responsible. "Believe me, I did. If he stole the food, he either ate it or cached it somewhere because he doesn't have it. There's nothing else to be done about it, and we're wasting precious energy worrying about it. Let's focus on getting some fresh meat, okay?"

The men nodded in a grim fashion and trudged off to fetch their guns.

Buck sensed eyes on him, the hair on the back of his neck standing on end. With a quick movement he turned.

Sinclair.

The man stood a few feet behind him with a strangely dilated gaze. Buck let out a breath and took a step toward him.

Sinclair shrieked and held out a quivering hand that said stop.

Buck took another step. "I just want to talk to you."

Sinclair drew out a long, wicked-looking knife.

Where had he gotten that? Buck stopped. "I'm not going to hurt you. It's okay. Just put down the knife."

The knife shook in Sinclair's hand as the big man stared unseeing into Buck's eyes. Suddenly Sinclair turned and rushed toward the camp, running as fast as his stocky legs could carry him.

Buck ran after him, but the man was surprisingly fast. The men around the camp scattered as he rushed into their midst. One pulled out a gun and another grabbed Buck's gun and tossed it to him. They all stopped and stared at Sinclair as he slowed to a disjointed jog, looking lost and baffled.

Ellen was just coming over a small rise back toward camp with an armful of wood. Sinclair must have seen her first as he changed directions and charged toward her. She couldn't see him! The wood was stacked as high as the top of her head on one side, the side Sinclair was approaching from.

Buck shot off toward them. "Ellen! Stay back!"

She dropped the wood and looked around her, but it was too late. Sinclair pinned her arms down from behind with one hand while the other held the knife under her chin.

Ellen held perfectly still as Buck neared, slow and cautious now. "Come on, man. You don't want to hurt Ellen. She's been so kind to you, kind to all of us, remember?"

Sinclair didn't move or say a word in acknowledgment.

"We're almost to Dawson. Don't give up! You can make it!"

A small light of recognition flashed in Sinclair's eyes. He hesitated, swayed; the knife wavered in his hand.

Buck used the moment to full advantage, striking with coiled speed born from his fear for Ellen. He rushed Sinclair and slammed down on the arm holding the weapon with bone-crushing strength.

The knife flew some distance and sank into the snow where one of the men rushed to grab it. Sinclair fell back as Ellen fell forward into Buck's arms.

Buck, his breath coming harsh from between his teeth, pointed his gun at Sinclair, resisting the very strong urge to pull the trigger. He was about to order Sinclair be tied up, but the man collapsed over his knees and was sobbing like a baby.

"I'm sorry. I won't do it again. I don't know what came over me." He looked at Buck with wide, earnest eyes.

Ellen grasped Buck's collar. "It's okay. Let him go. He's just afraid."

Buck gazed down into Ellen's pleading eyes and gave a short nod. "Stay away from him though, okay?"

Ellen nodded, her eyes grim with all the truth of what this march was uncovering in all of them.

She walked back to the knot of observing men as Buck walked up and held out a hand toward Sinclair. "Get up, soldier! It's time to march!"

Sinclair stared up at him with a tear-soaked face, tears that had frozen into tracks of crackling ice, but his eyes had returned to normal. He took Buck's hand, stood, his gaze darting sheepishly around at the group.

"All right, then." Buck turned toward the onlookers. "Let's get to Dawson, shall we?"

Chapter Four

"We're close. Keep moving!" Buck motioned us forward, his face set in unyielding lines of survival.

I glanced over at him and tried to hide my very real fear. Sometimes when I blinked, my eyes refused to focus for a few seconds. When I leaned my head to one side or the other to take the next trudging step, dizziness flooded me. I didn't say anything to Buck, but I knew he had noticed. He stayed closer than ever by my side and glanced at me often.

Toward evening I was swaying with exhaustion. When Buck stopped, I tried to stop with him, but my legs buckled in a half movement of stopping and continuing forward as I had done all day.

Buck caught me and pulled me in close. His strength was less than the other time he had held me in his arms, but he was still core strong as he demanded in my ear, "Fight Ellen. I can't lose you too."

I didn't know if I could do it. The sting of snow-wind, needle sharp and biting, lacerated my face. I looked away from him, looked farther ahead at the miles upon miles of nothing but rolling white. Above me black buzzards circled, eternally patient in nature's ability to deliver their dinner. My breath came in pants. My heart pounded against the cage of my ribs, against the thin layer of flesh that stood between me and the arctic cold.

"Can you keep going?"

I nodded but wasn't sure I believed it.

Buck called for the troops to continue.

The men were close on my heels as I was on Buck's. The sleds cut the path through ten inches of top powder. Their rudders and paw prints made a rough path but better than anything my shaking leg muscles could do. Hunched-up backs and clawing feet—I loved those dogs.

So cold.

The thought protruded again, but I tried to shake it off, create some kind of shield where it would hit, fall to the ground unrecognized. My breath froze against my chin and cheeks and crackled there when I pressed my numb lips together. The moccasins were doing their work as I could still feel my feet . . . but the rest of me? I couldn't feel anything save the blink of my eyes against unknown depths of exhaustion. We were climbing uphill now.

I must have fallen behind.

I don't remember seeing the dark coats of the men in our party passing me. I didn't remember falling. But it was bliss.

Face-first in a fluffy death.

I turned my head out of the snow, rolled over, and stared at the darkening sky. Each day seemed shorter than the last, just as my life, spiraling down to that final dark moment. A smile froze upon my face. "Jonah, are you there?"

A little laugh escaped my chest, and then I coughed and coughed.

When the spasms stopped, I spread my arms out wide and peered heavenward. *Is he there, Lord? Will I see him now? Is he finally whole?*

I closed my eyes and imagined heaven. I imagined pearly gates and the face of Jesus and then, as I drifted into a nether land between here and there, lost and forgotten images played across my mind. I drew in a big breath, and the cold shot all the way to my head. It lingered there, touching spots, awakening memories I'd long forgotten.

I saw Grandpa Ned and Nanna, how they used to come and whisk us away for a week or two in the summer months. I'd almost felt normal by the end of those visits. And then there was Christmas. They always came for a few precious days at Christmas. Nanna made Jonah and me gingerbread and hot cocoa and then every evening told us stories about her life and our mother's life before . . . when she was happy. And Grandpa took us out to find the perfect Christmas tree. Sometimes the jolly sound would even coax my mother from her room.

My chest shook in a violent spasm, and I didn't know if it was the cold or the memory that was so real.

Mother had walked with a stilted gait, as if each step might bring some disaster. I rushed forward and grasped her arm, so frail and thin I wondered that I couldn't see right through her, and helped her to the scrabbly green chair by the Christmas tree.

She smiled down at me, making my heart so happy I thought it would burst from my chest. I hung by her chair offering to fetch her sweets, laughing too loud at something Nanna said, and cavorting with Jonah.

Then it happened. "I need to go lie back down, Ellen. You and Jonah quiet down now."

I watched her retreating figure with a growing hole in the middle of my chest—torn, ripped, ragged, bleeding. I sank to the floor and stared at the Christmas tree.

Christmas. Who needed it? My father left us right before Christmas. Everything changed at Christmas.

"Get her out! Get her on her feet!"

The voice was familiar, but I couldn't rouse the energy to care. My body was hefted, raised upright. My head fell toward my right shoulder and bobbed up and down as they heaved me to my feet.

"Walk, Ellen. You have to get your heart pumping!"

The voice was so familiar. It had a warm feeling to it that lent my heart a spark. I wanted to grasp that spark, hold it in my hands, and blow life on it, but I didn't have the energy, only smiles. I smiled at the voice. I tried to laugh, but the sound came out hoarse and rasping, the cold snatching away my voice.

They propped me up—who I did not know. They took my arms and wrapped them around shaking shoulders and marched me.

My legs wobbled like a newborn calf. Half dragging me and half stumbling, we plowed through the frozen deep. My breath came fast now, and then a strange anxiety rushed through my body making it hum with energy. Every nerve began to tingle.

I had almost died! I wanted to *live!*

As the blood flowed through my veins, I felt the need to push my feet against the ground and walk. I gritted my teeth against the cold and the pain and panted with the effort to bring my body back to life.

Buck's harsh whisper was in my ear. He had been there at my side all along, saying the same thing over and over. "Don't give up. I can't lose you. Ellen! Ellen, do you hear me. Walk! Keep walking. Don't you dare give up!"

Some of the other men had built a fire, and as soon as I was able to stand on my own, Buck pushed me up close to it. If I had stood any closer, I would have singed off my eyelashes. Buck unbuttoned his coat and pulled me into his chest, me facing the fire with his determined strength at my back. He wrapped the sides of the fur-lined leather around me and leaned his head toward my neck, as if to take all of my cold into himself.

I pressed back into his chest, felt the warmth seep through my skin, and thought of ways to bind him to me. I couldn't help it. I craved commitment from a man like this—a man with a steady, unchanging nature. A man who would honor his promises. A man who would never, ever leave his wife and children at Christmastime.

There was only one problem—I wasn't that kind of woman. I'd left Jonah, abandoned my promise, and proved myself no better than *him*. I gazed, unseeing, into the roaring fire, feeling undeserving of the warmth that was bringing me back into the land of the living. The truth closed around my heart like a vise . . .

I was my father's daughter after all.

G battled with sleep that night. Death hovered around us like a thick fog. My dreams were awake and haunted. My body shivered in constant agony.

Buck pulled me in closer to his chest and wrapped his arm around my middle. Like the others we slept in sleeping furs close to the fire. Buck and I shared one and no one commented on it. I think the men were desperate enough to cuddle up to each other, but they opted for scooting as close to the fire as they dared. Every hour or so someone would get up and pile on more sticks and branches to keep the fire going all night. We were too cold to sleep soundly enough to let it die out.

"We're going to make it," Buck whispered next to my ear when the sounds of snoring from the men filled the night.

I nodded but was still afraid. Now, when I had every reason to live, it seemed the life force inside me was fading and there wasn't anything I could do about it. "Talk to me," I whispered, trying to hold back the panic. If I let myself drift off to sleep, I might never wake again.

Buck rubbed his hand up and down the length of my shivering arm. "What do you want to talk about?"

"Anything. Just keep talking to me. Please."

"Well, let's see. I left home when I was seventeen."

"That's young. Why?"

"My parents were corn farmers in Illinois. Pa expected that I would stick around and follow in his footsteps, but I wanted to see the world. My cousin Stephen and I decided to run off. He was eighteen so no one would think much about his disappearance, but I knew I would have to be gone awhile before I let my folks know I was okay or they would come after me."

"They must have been so worried." But another part of me thought it might have been wonderful. If I had left home at eighteen, my whole life would have been different. My mother hadn't tied me to my brother with a deathbed promise until I was nineteen.

"I felt a little bad about that, but I only let a few months go by and a lot of distance when I wrote to them. Stephen and I ended up in California, working on the docks, loading and unloading ships in San Francisco Bay. One day we were horsing around and decided to hide aboard one of them. Somehow we got bolted in an enclosed area in the cargo section of the hull. Next thing we knew, we were on our way to Brazil and then Argentina with a ship full of grain. What started as a lark turned into a five-year adventure on the high seas."

I thought of all the places he must have seen. It was hard for me to imagine such a carefree and adventurous life. "How did you end up in Alaska?"

"A ship." I could hear the smile in his voice. "Fish, sealskin, and whale blubber make a good export business. Stephen and I saved up enough money to buy our own ship, and then we headed for Alaska to set up our trading venture. We made friends with the Tlingit and other natives along the coast. In six more years we had a whole fleet of ships trading all over the world, and our company brought work to the struggling coastal villages. It turned out even better than we dreamed it would."

"Is that how you met your wife? In one of those villages?"

"Yes. When I first met her, she was sixteen and I was twenty-one. Her father asked that I wait two years before marrying her." His voice took on a faraway tone. "When I came to her village, she would run out to meet me with such exuberance, and then she would stop and look down, so shy, while I approached. It took a good while for me to get her to open up and talk, but . . . I just knew she was the one."

A stab of jealousy ripped through my stomach, surprising me with its intensity. The feeling was followed by shame. What right did I have to be jealous? None. "So you were married five years before she was killed."

"I will never forgive myself for taking her to Skagway with me. I knew the land was changing since the gold rush. I knew how dangerous it could be."

Buck's voice held all the bitterness of self-recrimination, and I could imagine the game of "what-ifs" he must have played over and over in his mind. "You couldn't have known what would happen, Buck." I tried to comfort him with soft words. "Where did you live?"

"We had a nice house in Sitka. I still do I guess, but I will probably sell it. I'm not sure where I will live after I find the man who shot her. I guess I'm a wanderer again."

I liked the idea that we were both wanderers, but I wasn't sure that I should. "I don't know where I will live either." My shivering had stopped, and I turned onto my back and looked up through the darkness at the pinpoints of starlight. Buck was facing me on his side with his head propped up on his hand, his eyes glinting like silver in sthe diffused light. I reached up and touched his cheek. "But I do know one thing."

"What's that?" His voice was pained and raspy.

"I'm glad to be alive. Thank you, Buck."

Inch by slow inch, he leaned toward me, and I thought he would kiss me, but there was enough light from the fire to see the battle raging in his eyes. His breath fanned across my face. I tilted my chin up in acquiescence, but he stopped, pulled back, and sighed.

"Good night, Ellen." He lay down as I turned back over and away from him, tears of disappointment stinging my eyes. He pulled me hard into his chest. "I'm sorry." He said it so low I had to strain to hear it. "I wish I could give you something. I want to."

"There is one thing I want," I whispered.

"What's that?"

"Christmas is coming. My father left us just before Christmas and—" The ache in my throat made words impossible for a few seconds.

Buck pulled me in tighter and leaned his face into my neck, waiting for me to continue.

"Now that Jonah is gone . . . I'll be alone this Christmas. Would you, could you, promise to be with me for that one day?" I turned my head toward his face and watched the play of emotions in his crystal blue eyes, knowing I was asking so much.

"I promise." His voice was gruff and low.

Joy seared my heart with a new kind of pain. "Thank you."

I tried to stay awake, exist in the feeling for as long as possible. I watched the pinpricks of light move with aching slowness across the sky, but I must have closed my eyes and allowed the exhaustion to overcome me.

For when we woke the next morning, Sinclair was gone.

Chapter Five

Fan out and search the perimeter of the camp," Buck instructed the men. "Sinclair may be close and still alive."

"Yeah, he was pretty shook up yesterday."

"His mind snapped, man," Zeke Robbins put in.

Buck nodded. "It's not uncommon in Alaska. Sometimes it's the cold, sometimes the constant darkness; the stress of this march has certainly played havoc on his mind."

George McCallister, the huge Scotsman of the group, said, "I don't feel sorry for him. Sinclair probably cached our food and is going back for it."

Buck's jaw tensed. "We don't know that for sure. If he's innocent and we didn't at least try and find him . . . Imagine it's you out there, and let's treat him as we would want to be treated."

"Is there anything I can do to help? I'm feeling better today." Ellen looked up at him with her big brown eyes full of disquiet, and Buck's heart lurched. He'd almost lost her yesterday. All he wanted to do was keep her close to his side.

"It's a good twenty degrees warmer today, thank God. That will make a big difference in how we all feel." His gaze darted over the camp. He pointed at the sleds. "You could help me hitch up the dogs and break down camp while the men search for Sinclair."

Ellen nodded and Buck led her over to where the dogs were clumped together under a tree. Poor fellows. They were tuckered out and only flopped their tails a couple of times as Ellen and he approached. Pride shot through

Buck as he looked them over. There had been many har-rowing moments on the trail, moments when he was break-ing the ice that formed over their nostrils, moments where they gazed at him with hunger bordering on panic making Buck wonder if they would go wild, moments when one or the other of them had slowed causing the rest of the pack to pull more of the load for a time so the weakest one could rest—all those moments when he'd prayed his dogs would make it.

He took a deep breath and closed his eyes as Blue's face nuzzled his. He gathered them around him with pats to their heads, backs, and sides, their tongues lolling, eyes brighter as they nudged to get closer to him.

After warming them up, he turned toward Ellen who was smiling tenderly at him and the dogs. The smile made his breath catch. He covered the sound by clearing his throat. "I'll show you how to hitch them to the sled."

He handed her a long leather strap. She grasped it, gazing up at him with that look she always gave him, like she believed in him, like she trusted him and thought he could do anything. It caught him off guard as it always did, made his heart strain to rise to the challenge—to be a better man than he was and deserve that look.

God, don't let me fail her like I failed my wife.

He paused to brush a stray curl back into her hood. The action made a knot form in his throat. What was he doing? He'd always done that with his wife—brushed back her hair into its tight braid—but Ellen's hair was different, like a waterfall of silk. The color was a deeper brown than her eyes, strands rich with chestnut hues of brown and almost black. His fingertips brushed across her reddened cheek before his hand fell to his side.

A part of him wanted to turn and walk away. An equally strong part wanted to kiss her. He ground his teeth together. *Kalage has only been gone seven months. What's wrong with you? Get a hold of yourself.*

His voice was gruff, but he couldn't help it as he turned toward the dogs and instructed, "Put the harness around their shoulders and chests, then we will hitch them to the sleds."

Ellen hesitated when the first dog grew restless under her unsure hands. Feeling that he had his emotions under control, Buck walked over and petted Shelby. "It will help if you know their names. Let's introduce you. This is Shelby, the lead dog. She is strong and never forgets a thing. We can take a trail one time and Shelby will remember it. I have never been lost with her as my lead." He patted Shelby on the head.

"How do you know the dogs so well? I thought they came from the steamer."

"These four and this sled are mine. I brought them with me from Sitka. That's how Kalage and I traveled to Skagway."

"Oh." She looked sorry to have brought it up.

Ruffling the fur on the neck of the next dog, Buck motioned Ellen farther down the line. "This is Duke; he's what we call the swing dog. He helps the other dogs follow Shelby's lead." He patted him twice on his side. "Very strong. Pretty tuckered out now, though, aren't you, boy?"

Duke panted up into Buck's face and then licked his hand, as if to assure Buck he was up to the task.

Buck moved to the next dog, a little smaller and darker. "This is Gunsmoke. He's a good musher, puts all of his efforts into it. He has a heart of gold."

Gunsmoke nuzzled into Buck's hand and wagged his tail with an energy that spoke of love stronger than exhaustion.

"And last is Blue. She's the youngest, just three years old, but she's strong, and I think she has the makings of a leader in her."

"She's beautiful." Ellen reached out and petted Blue's silky head.

"She's a full-blooded Malamute. The others are huskies except for Gunsmoke and he's a mix." Buck grinned. "Wouldn't surprise me if he had some wolf in him."

Buck finished tightening the harness on Shelby just as Randy broke through a stand of trees and hurried toward them. The look on his face wasn't good.

"What is it, Randy? Did you find something?" Buck asked.

Randy glanced at Ellen and then said in a terse voice, "I found Sinclair."

"Alive?"

Randy shook his head. "He'd been . . . half eaten. A bear, maybe. There were lots of tracks around him."

Ellen covered her mouth with her hand, and Buck bit off a low curse. "That's too bad," Buck muttered instead. His mouth hardened into a thin line. "Bear meat isn't the tastiest dinner, but we could sure do with some fresh meat. Do you think it might be close by?"

Randy shrugged. He had never been one of the hunters. "That's what took me so long. I tracked the prints for a little ways, but I didn't want to go too far alone. Should we send out a hunting party?"

Buck gazed at the group as he deliberated. If the hunters were successful, they might gain the strength to make it to Dawson. If they weren't, they would lose valuable time and energy, making the likelihood of success a dim possibility. Buck drew out his compass, studied it, and then stared at the sky. It didn't look like snow, but there was that gut feeling, tingling, warning him. Buck's gaze lingered on Ellen's face, his mouth tight and grim.

"I think a storm might be approaching. We don't have time to waste. Let's keep moving."

It was midafternoon when Buck suddenly stopped and pointed. "Look!" He waved us toward him. We all stopped, each seeing it at the same time, each comprehending our salvation: Dawson City. A great cry leapt from our throats. Some of the men whooped while others fell to their knees in thanksgiving. One by one we fell apart—laughing and cheering, hugging one another with ice tears freezing on our cheeks. One by one we gave way to our hope.

I looked down at my snow-covered moccasins, then up into Buck's glad eyes. "Will the snow really melt?"

Buck grasped my hand. "And the ice too." His voice had a quiver in it as he gazed deep and full into my eyes.

Tears sprang to my throat as I smiled up at him in hope that someday the ice around my heart would melt too. "Yes. The ice too."

We rushed forward with renewed energy and stumbling steps. The smile that was pasted across my frozen lips didn't waver over the next half hour as Dawson turned from a dark spot on the horizon into the shapes of buildings and then scurrying townsfolk. As word spread, scores of people rushed from tents, shops, and saloons to greet us.

I walked down the hard-packed, snow-clogged Front Street holding tight to Buck's side, but we were soon separated as curious men and a few women squeezed between us. Their questions sounded like distant buzzing in my ears. I looked into the faces of bearded men dressed in all manner of winter gear and swayed with exhaustion.

A woman's arms came around to steady me as I started to collapse to the street. She held me upright for a moment with her hands on my upper arms.

I started to thank her but could only gape at her beauty. She was dressed in the most stunning gown I had ever seen. Bright red with black lace trim, cut low in the front, and a full skirt adorned with more black lace. A fur wrap hung slightly askew, as if hastily thrown over her shoulders.

When I gazed back at her face, she was smiling at me with a knowing look. Her hair was a shocking red, fat rows of curls piled atop her head and spilling down her back. She was the most outlandish and beautiful creature I had ever seen.

She stretched out a perfect, ivory hand. "I'm Kate, Queen of Dawson."

Dawson had a queen? I knew we were in Canada now but hadn't imagined a queen. I smiled, a feeble motion of my lips, and shook her hand. "Ellen Pierce." I was suddenly, horribly aware of how awful I must appear.

Her smile grew, flashing perfect pearls of teeth. "I would like to ask you all sorts of questions, but you look frozen through and starving to boot. Do you have a place to stay?"

I turned and saw that Buck was surrounded by a large group of men. He seemed to be explaining our situation.

Kate's eyes followed mine. Her gaze held appreciation mixed with humor. "Is that your husband?" Her voice had a faint accent I didn't recognize.

I blushed and shook my head. "He's our leader. Buck Lewis."

"Hmmm." She nodded and searched the crowd. Her perfect brow puckered. The frown only made her seem prettier somehow, as if that look could win her anything she wanted. Her blue eyes flashed back at me, and she rushed out the words. "Old Mrs. Lawrence is about to descend upon us. She'll offer you a room, of course, and you should probably take it, though she'll charge you an outrageous fee as soon as you get on your feet."

She cocked her head and studied me for a moment and then seemed to come to some conclusion. "Or you could stay with me. I'll not ask anything of you, but I won't say I won't offer an . . . opportunity or two when you are feeling better."

"An opportunity?" Dizziness swept over me in a wave. Did the beautiful creature have any idea just how hard it was for my sluggish brain to try and decipher what she was saying?

"Never mind." Kate drew me close to her side. "We'll say you are my cousin. Just don't hate me for it later."

How I could ever hate her was beyond me.

The woman she spoke of barreled toward us and then stopped short when she saw Kate's arm around my waist supporting me. She huffed, her gaze not quite looking at either of us.

"Mrs. Lawrence," Kate voice took on a purring quality. "This is my cousin come all the way from . . ."

"California." I filled in the blank.

Kate nodded happily. "I can barely believe she made it, but we'll have to hear the tale later. She is about to drop, as you can see. I should take her home."

The worn-out-looking woman pressed her lips together in a thin line, gave me a long studying glare, and then turned her back on us.

Well, I wouldn't want to stay with her anyway.

"Quite so," Kate muttered, and I realized I must have said it aloud. "Do you want to say anything to your friends?"

Buck was surrounded by townspeople and speaking to them. His face appeared ashen with exhaustion. I wanted to shout at them to leave him alone but didn't have the

strength. "No, just some water, a warm fire, and a real bed."
How did I get so lucky to have such a beautiful guardian
angel to help me?

"Of course." She waved toward a group of men who
disengaged from the crowd and walked over to us. "This
here is Ben Roseland. Ben, could you or one of your associ-
ates carry my new friend here? I don't think she will make
it another step without some help."

I was about to protest when strong arms scooped me
up, making my head spin anew. The man had cheery, hazel
eyes and a broad chest and shoulders. I decided to stay put.
He seemed more than capable of the task and ready to do
anything Kate asked of him.

I peered back over Ben's shoulder as Buck looked up.
Our gazes locked for a long moment. I waved, my arm feeling like a well-cooked noodle. He frowned but was unable
to do anything to get to me. I could find him later. Maybe
he would be staying with Mrs. Lawrence. A bubble of hys-
terical laughter escaped my throat.

Ben looked down and grinned at me. "Nice ride?"

"Oh yes. Very comfortable, thank you," I managed to choke out, wanting to laugh again. Maybe I was just so happy to be alive. I don't think I really believed we would make it to Dawson, but we had, and it felt wonderful to know these people, these larger-than-life, glittering strangers, were more than willing to take care of me.

I closed my eyes and sighed. Dawson was a very nice place indeed.

Chapter Six

I awoke to the quiet ticking of a clock. My eyelids were as heavy as sodden blankets. I tried to lift them, felt a wave of exhaustion overwhelm me, and then drifted back into the darkness.

I don't know how much longer it was until I had the next coherent thought, but it came stronger, brighter. The sun was loud against my eyes.

I blinked and then blinked again. Where was I?

The first thing I saw was a flowing, silken canopy draped above the bed. It was white, translucent, and fluttered with the soft air moving in the room. I turned my head toward a white marble fireplace ablaze with warm heat. The mantel held a vase of what appeared to be real flowers, but how that could be in the dead of winter in a town so far from anywhere was puzzling and a little frightening. I sniffed the air and smelled an odd mix of roses and . . . metal.

My brow furrowed. Metal? I had never smelled metal. Well, that wasn't entirely true. A memory surged forward. Jonah holding a gold nugget in his palm. He pressed it to my nose, forcing my head toward his hand, as he told me of our next plan, our next city, our next escape from reality. The name, the vision of him—my dark, glorious, insane brother—brought back the truth. He'd died on the trail. I had let him die.

I'd *wanted* him to die.

As the thoughts connected around my sleep-clouded brain, a sob rushed from my rib cage. What had I done? I'd failed in everything my mother had charged me with. I had not kept him safe. I had not protected him from the harsh realities of the world. I had not been nailed to my cross to the bitter end. No. I'd done what Christ had not. I had plucked out the nails as soon as the opportunity presented itself. Yes, I had spilled out the last five years for Jonah, but I had not gone the full distance.

I'd chosen my life before his.

The thought made me want to sink back into the blackness of sleep and stay there forever, but my body rebelled. It fought toward full consciousness and embraced the bright light seeping through the window.

The door creaked open. I turned my head to see a woman holding a tray with something steaming atop it. She had a smile I recognized in a vague way. And her hair. It was so very red.

"Hello again, Ellen."

My gaze followed her as she set the tray on the bedside table.

"You've finally rejoined the land of the living. And about time too. I was getting weary of spooning broth into your mouth." She laughed then, a tinkling of bells in the room. I blinked at her, still trying to wake up.

She busied herself by propping me up with a strong arm and plumping my pillows so I could sit up. A few seconds later I heard tea being poured into a delicate cup. She pressed it toward me, helping my hand reach for the handle. The steam drifted toward my nose and smelled like heaven.

"How long have I been here?" I croaked out, taking a tiny sip.

"Three days now. You roused every few hours, and we spooned nourishment into you when we could." Kate looked down toward my feet. "We were afraid frostbite had taken your toes, but I am glad to say they are as pretty as ever thanks to Doc Maynard. He's a friend and it's a good thing. The other doctor in town—" She shivered and I understood that Doc Maynard had saved my feet.

The sugary tea slid down my throat and warmed my stomach. Kate lifted a bowl from the tray, handed it to me, and took the empty cup, holding it loosely in her lap. "The color is coming back into your cheeks," she commented as I took a long swallow of the brown broth.

Nothing had ever tasted so good. I nodded above the bowl. "Thank you." It was all I could say. I didn't know how to tell her she wasn't real to me yet.

She was like some fairy queen come to life in her bright yellow dress with a wide green sash tied into a giant bow at her back. From her ears dangled what appeared like yellow diamonds and a matching three-stranded choker wrapped around her neck. Who was she?

I realized, in a sudden yet slow way, that I was ensconced in the finest satin bedding. I gazed about the room as I sipped my broth, each glance a new revelation. The silken wall coverings, paintings that could have belonged in a renowned museum, glittering golden molding around windows and encircling the ceiling. Above my head a huge chandelier hung suspended. It glittered with cut crystal, the beams of sunlight from the window catching and splitting into dots of colored light that danced around the room. It was a fairy place . . . but we were in Dawson City. A tent city from all accounts. A place where the newly rich rubbed elbows with the down-and-out. Kate was definitely not one of the down-and-out.

"You have had several visitors, Ellen."

I wiped my chin on the cloth she handed me. "Who?"

"Buck was here yesterday." She smiled a little when she said his name, and a thought, unbidden, came to mind that they would make a perfect couple. "He tried to move you," she waved a delicate hand in the air as if brushing away an annoying fly, "to some boardinghouse he'd found for you. But I convinced him you were in no shape to be moved just yet and that it should be your decision where you stay, now that your horrid trek is over, don't you agree?"

I didn't know what to say to that. "I guess so." I hadn't really thought much about what I would do after reaching Dawson City, but the thought of not seeing Buck . . . What if he had already left Dawson? "Is Buck still in town?" The man he was tracking might not even be in this town any longer. Panic washed over me as I rose from the pillow and tried to swing my legs over the side of the bed.

Kate stopped me with a touch on my arm, her eyes soft and kind. "Shh. It's all right. I told him to come back in a few days. You need to rest."

I leaned back against the pillow with a long sigh. I was so tired, more tired than I ever remembered being. "Thank you," I said again, not knowing how else to tell her how grateful I was.

"No need for that. You'll be as good as new in a few more days. And then you have to tell me—"

"Tell you?"

"Your story, of course." She patted the blanket and then fixed it around me. "I will know everything. And I will tell you everything I know. And then we will be the best of friends." Her face turned wistful. "I know it."

For a second, just a tiny moment of time, her face lost its facade, softened, and surprise flooded me as I glimpsed the smallest peek into her soul. The queen of Dawson, a woman who appeared to have everything . . . was lonely.

"Yes. We will be friends." I agreed and then wondered if I should have.

What *was* that strange noise?

I gave up trying to sleep, swung my legs over the side of the enormous bed, and let my toes dangle above the frosty floor. I cocked my head, heard it again, and furrowed my brow. It sounded like the deep tones of male laughter combined with feminine gasping, and it was coming from the room next door.

I stepped into the slippers Kate had so thoughtfully loaned me, then shuffled toward the door, turned the knob, and peeked out. The hallway was dark and quiet, but light shone from the crack underneath each and every closed door, six counting the room I had been given. I paused, a sense of unease coming over me, and vacillated between discovering the truth or heading back to bed and burying my head beneath my comfortable, downy pillow.

Taking a logical approach, I ticked off the facts before me on my fingers:

> One: The house was very large, much larger than I had realized when that young man carried me here.

Two: Kate was wealthy. The house was more palatial than anything I had ever seen in more civilized country, and it would require a great deal of wealth and connections to have such fine things so far from anywhere.

Three: Kate may or may not own this house—of that I wasn't sure. If she didn't, who did it belong to and how was Kate connected to them?

Four: The sounds, quieter here in the hall, had a ring of something . . . well, pleasurable, and while I knew I should mind my own business, something told me this might influence my future. And then . . .

Five: Kate's words on the icy street the day we'd arrived niggled at the back of my mind. Hadn't she said something like, "I will take you home but don't hate me for it later"? What did that mean?

The feeling in the pit of my stomach grew, and I began to feel nauseated. I tiptoed to the door next to my room and pressed my ear against the wood.

As soon as my weight shifted against the door, it swung open and then bumped with a loud bang against the far wall. I fell forward from the lack of expected support and landed, sprawling, on my stomach on a very nice, soft rug.

The sounds in the room came to an abrupt stop. There was some rustling of covers and then Kate's familiar voice. "Ellen? Good heavens, what are you doing?"

I looked up, heat rising to my face. My gaze swung to the man in the bed with her and then darted away. It was Randy Olsen from our group and . . . and . . . he was sitting up in the bed—shirtless! His mouth dropped open as he recognized me. My gaze swung away from his white face.

I heard Kate slip into a dressing gown and come around the bed. "Here, let me help you up." She reached for my arm.

I shook my head and scurried to stand, turning away from the scene. My voice came out in a mortified squeak. "I am so sorry, Kate." I kept my gaze locked to the floor as I fled the room.

Kate followed me a little ways. "Was there something you needed? Are you all right?"

I shook my head. I was not all right but couldn't begin to put into words my shock. How had I not known? How, with everything so obvious, had I not guessed?

I was being housed in a brothel!

And a very successful one at that.

I shut the door and leaned back against it, my breathing coming in gasps. I had to get out of here. The townspeople . . . Mrs. Lawrence's disapproving look . . . Buck's surprised look! It all came back to me. That I had agreed, and so readily, to go home with Kate put me square in the category of a prostitute in their eyes. Well, Buck would know the truth, wouldn't he? He would know I would never stoop to such a thing.

I took a calming breath. Hadn't Kate said all the men of our little expedition had come to visit me? Randy's face and thin white chest rose in my mind's view. Visit her, more likely. Revulsion filled me. Men! Barely on their feet and the first place they go—

My eyes widened. What if Buck had been here to see Kate or one of the other girls who must live and do business here? What if checking on me was a side thought too?

No. I couldn't let myself think like that. Buck was better than that. Never mind that he was hunting his wife's killer. He would turn him over to the law when he found him, right? But what if he took revenge himself? What might happen to him then? I pushed away from the door as the turmoil of my thoughts swirled through my mind.

My next thought was to pack my things and get out of this place, but my pack was still on the dogsled, wherever that might be. The only person who knew where it was located was Buck. I had nothing here but the clothes I had arrived in.

I stepped over to the ornate bureau where I had seen a young maid—a very pretty young girl I reminded myself with a shiver—put away my clothes. They were in the top drawer, folded in neat squares among other fine white blouses. I shook them out, hearing nothing from the other side of the wall anymore, thank heaven, and then hurried into them.

I was buttoning the pearl buttons when the realization struck me that it was late at night and I didn't have any idea where to begin my search for Buck. It would be foolish to go out this time of night alone, but I could hardly stay here. As I contemplated what to do next, my hands shook against the buttons, and I couldn't push them through the holes.

A knock on the door had me turning around. I smoothed down my skirt, still wearing Kate's satin blue slippers, and croaked out, "Who is it?"

"Ellen, it's me, Kate. Can we talk?"

I didn't want to talk to her. Kate had a way of making things look fine and good when they weren't. I'd imagined her as my guardian angel, but she'd proven to be . . . well . . . I wasn't exactly sure what she was, but it was not that. "I'm trying to sleep, Kate. Can we talk in the morning?" I tried to make my voice sound unconcerned and tired.

A brief pause ensued, and then a sniffle and a sigh came from the other side of the door. "Well, I suppose. Just don't do anything rash. Please, promise me. Let me at least have a chance to explain."

My heart unbent a bit, but my mind demanded, *What was there to explain?* Suddenly I was angrier than I had ever been. I walked over and jerked open the door. Kate was just turning away, but she turned back, a light of pleading in her eyes.

"You should have told me."

"Might I come in? We don't want to wake the others."

"Are they sleeping?" I asked, incredulous at her lie.

"Well, perhaps not," Kate had the decency to look embarrassed, "but I would rather talk to you without listening ears."

I stepped back and allowed her graceful figure to float across the threshold. It was hard to believe she was a fallen woman, a madam of prostitutes. She was just so . . . perfect. I steeled myself against her charm and shut the door. Turning toward her, I pressed my lips together and folded my arms in front of my chest. "Well?"

She clasped her hands together in front of her silky robe. "Oh, dear, you are upset, aren't you?"

"Upset?" I hissed. "How could you have plucked me off the street like that, knowing I didn't understand, knowing how weak I was? You didn't even give me a choice!"

"That's hardly fair, Ellen. I gave you a choice when Mrs. Lawrence was walking toward us, remember? I said she would demand repayment for her kindness when you were better and that I would demand nothing of you." She paused, her eyes intent. "Have I not taken the very best care of you? Have I demanded anything in return?"

I hesitated. "Not yet, but I remember you saying something about opportunities? Tell me you don't want me trapped here. That was your plan all along, wasn't it?" I pressed my lips into the tightest line I could manage.

Kate shrugged a delicate shoulder and looked at me askance. "It was a possibility, of course. You are very pretty, and I knew you would have a successful run in one of my establishments."

"Your establishments?" The fact that it was plural didn't escape me.

"That's where you don't quite understand, dear. I own several saloons, two dance halls, and this"—she held out a hand, her gaze skittering across the decadent room, satisfaction resting on her curved lips—"the Red Feather, the most lavish and upscale brothel in Dawson, if not the whole country. I'm not asking you to become like me." She shook her head a little and her long, red curls bounced upon her shoulder. "Once you were well, I would have offered you one of several opportunities. A pretty woman is rarer than gold nuggets around here." She appraised me with a tight smile. "I am a very successful businesswoman. You can't blame me for wanting to snatch you up first."

I stood there, rooted to the floor, not knowing what to think. "I planned to buy a claim and pan for gold." It was a half-thought-through plan. On the trail I didn't think of much beyond making it to Dawson. Now I would have to figure out what my future would be without my brother.

Kate tossed back her head and laughed. "Oh, I am sure I could arrange for that too, but I don't think you understand the, ah, difficulties up here. You would have to endure weeks of camping in the ice and snow to hold down your claim. Then as the creek bed thaws, you would be standing in freezing water up to your knees while your back aches from holding that heavy gold pan." She smiled again, as if explaining something elementary to a beloved child. "You would have a much better chance striking it rich in another line of work, any other line of work, let me assure you."

The picture of the hardships of panning for gold validated my worst fears. I had always had a delicate, weaker frame, as had Jonah. I'd wondered when he decided we should come here how the two of us would have the necessary strength for such work, and that was before I'd discovered the bitter temperatures. The thought of going back out into the frozen tundra and slogging through icy rivers put a true shiver of foreboding up my spine. But I couldn't stay here. There was no question about that. As my mind whirled with possible solutions, a timid knock sounded at the door.

Kate opened it to a hastily dressed Randy Olsen standing on the threshold, turning his felt hat round and round in his hands.

"Not now, Mr. Olsen," Kate hissed. "I told you I would refund your money in a few minutes."

Randy's face reddened, and his head bobbed at me, but he avoided my eyes. "It's not that, ma'am." He dug in his pocket and pulled out a piece of paper, which he held out toward me. "I have a message for Miss Pierce. I was, uh, going to leave it for her before I left."

Kate reached for the note, but I hurried over and grabbed it from her delicate fingers. "Thank you, Mr. Olsen." I turned away and opened the letter.

Dear Ellen,

I have received word that the man who shot my wife and his cohort have left Dawson City and are traveling up one of the tributaries of the Yukon River. I plan to leave first thing in the morning to track them. I regret that I must leave so soon, but if I am to find them before winter truly sets in, I have no choice. If you are able, please meet me at the warehouse (#42 on Front Street), where I have stored our packs and the sleds. I will be readying my team by seven o'clock.

I would like to discuss your future plans so you can be moved from your present location. If I don't see you in the morning, I will leave some money for you at the Bodega Hotel where I am staying. Just ask for it at the front desk. But I do hope to see you, Ellen. Please come.

Yours,
Buck

I turned back toward Kate and Randy, both silent and staring, with the note clutched to my chest. He was leaving! And so soon! I took a long breath. "Thank you for bringing the note, Randy. If you see Buck, please tell him I will be there in the morning."

"Where are you going?" Kate looked alarmed.

"I'm leaving in the morning. I have to see Buck, and then I will find another place to stay."

She started to speak, but I raised my hand. "Thank you for your care, Kate. I really do appreciate it, but it's time."

Kate sniffed and I was surprised by how genuinely upset she looked as she rapidly blinked and pressed one hand against her chest. She sighed, though, and gave me a brief nod. "I suppose so." She turned toward Randy and started to usher him from the room. "Well, get some sleep, my dear. It sounds as if you have a busy day ahead of you tomorrow."

I took a step forward and then another.

She stopped and turned at the door. "Good night, Ellen."

I gave her a small smile. "Good-bye, Kate."

Chapter Seven

even o'clock. It was time.

I ignored the curious glances of the towns-
folk as I trudged through six inches of new
snow down Front Street toward the ware-
house on the white bank of the Yukon River. The cold and
the miseries of the trail washed back over me as I sucked
in the freezing air. How could Buck face going back out
there? And alone this time? More important, was there any
way to talk him out of it?

The warehouse was easy to spot, painted a pale yellow and sitting beside a wharf full of ice-locked boats. There were hundreds of them in all shapes and sizes. My gaze scanned the homemade crafts as I walked up the cleared path to the door. Who were all these people? What were their lives like? What were their stories and what had brought them here?

Making my way to the front door, I noted the deep snowdrift on either side and signs of Buck, the footprints I had followed and knew so well. A pang of longing stopped me, shocking in its intensity.

I longed to see his face—sure, intense, and purpose filled. I longed to see his eyes and the way he looked at me as if we were the only two people on earth, as if no one mattered to him as much as I did. I longed for the current of understanding between us that was instant and as natural as breath. I longed to touch his hands and his face, feel the whiskers of his beard rub rough under my fingertips. Most of all, I longed to hear his voice telling me he would stay and that . . .

I took a deep breath and pushed open the door.

It swung shut behind me leaving me in semidarkness. The place smelled of freshly sawed lumber and hay. Bales of livestock feed were stacked in rows to the ceiling against one wall. A light came from around a corner and a faint noise. I picked my way around piles of crates and various boxes, clumps of snow dripping from my moccasins and turning to slush around my feet. I came around the corner and saw him.

Buck's back was to me, and I watched, unnoticed, as he sorted the packs from one of the dogsleds. He stacked them in a pile and anything belonging to him—his pack, sleeping furs, tarp, dog harnesses—in another pile.

I held my breath as he lifted my pack. He held it for a long moment, leaning his head over it, appearing to be weighing a decision. His neck and shoulders stiffened, and he sighed before he set it down with aching slowness on the ground, away from his pile but not quite in the other pile either.

Tears stung my eyes. "I wish I could go with you, Buck."

He turned toward me, a startled movement of his head and shoulders. "Ellen." His voice was colored with surprise and pleasure. The sound of my name on his lips made my heart flutter with a heady feeling.

"You came." He walked over and pulled me into his arms.

I reached up and grasped the edges of his jacket, burying my face in his neck. He smelled of creeks and rivers crossed, of mountains scaled, of snow and clean, sharp fir trees, the perfect mix of man and nature. Why couldn't he belong to me forever?

"Don't go." My voice was so low I didn't know if he heard me.

He held me close, kissing the top of my head as his hands came up to grip the sides of my face. With gentle pressure he tilted my head back until I was looking into his clean-shaven, rugged, beautiful face. His gaze roved over my features—eyes and eyebrows, nose and cheeks, my lips—like a whispered caress.

Tension coursed through me as his gaze locked with mine. I saw the internal battle raging within him. And I saw the pain of his answer before he said it.

"I have to."

"But it's so dangerous. Can't you track them later? Come spring?"

Buck just stared at me, and I knew the answer was as solid as stone in his heart. No amount of begging would change that. Nausea turned my stomach.

He would leave. He would never come back. I would never see him again.

He didn't make any promises. But he did pull me hard against him as his lips came down on mine.

It wasn't what I had expected a kiss to be. I imagined it to be hard, a pressure that bowed me back and made me feel . . . taken over. But Buck's lips were gentle and firm at the same time. They moved over mine—inviting, coaxing, exploring—as if he would give as much as he could and expected that I do the same.

I pressed toward him with equal intent. My hands clung to his broad shoulders as I breathed him in, wanting more, wanting it to last. Knowing that it wouldn't last made a bit-tersweet ache fill my heart. Tears spilled out and slid down to traverse the paths his fingers made across my cheeks.

He moved his hands to my throat and kissed my tears, drinking them into himself, and then my heart squeezed as he settled his forehead against mine, both of us breathing hard in the stillness of the room.

I wanted to beg again. I wanted to demand he give me a chance and let his wife rest in peace, but I could feel the turmoil within him and knew he did not have peace enough for that decision. So I decided to savor the moment we did have and not ruin it with wanting more.

My lashes felt wet against the rounded curve of my cheeks as I closed my eyes and nestled back into his neck, my arms wrapped around him too tight for him not to know what I was thinking. He didn't pull back. He held me against him, kissed my head and the side of my face, and then my lips again.

I was glad I had never kissed another. I was glad he was the one I first loved.

When we broke apart, we looked a bit sheepishly at each other. Buck cleared his throat. "Would you like to help me sort through this mess? I'll need someone to find the others and return their packs to them." The determination in his voice to get back to the business of leaving was another slap of reality.

"I can do that." My voice sounded stronger than I felt.

It didn't take long to get to the bottom of the pile. Jonah's pack was the last one. Compassion filled Buck's eyes as he passed it into my arms.

Jonah, my brother. I clutched his pack to my chest, feeling it ache like a wound that wouldn't heal. His face was the first image I saw in the morning, taking a moment for me to remember that I didn't have to rush to his side to discover if it would be a good day where his smile was light, his mind clear, or a dark day where he accused me of plotting to leave him and heard whispered voices of torture. His face was the last image I saw before succumbing to sleep; guilt, remorse, regret—a new blanket that covered me each night.

His pack was as heavy as stone. I opened it, upended it, let the life of my brother pour onto the floor around me. There were his pants, so narrow at the waist but still requiring the rope belt he'd had to keep them up. His best shirt, a bright blue and his favorite. I remembered when I had bought it for him and how his pleased smile made my heart surge with love for him. I held the shirt up to my face and inhaled, closing my eyes and seeing him at his best. I knelt and looked down, my hand skimming the pile of the remains of his short life.

My hand met with a hard edge. I picked it up, unwrapped the large bundle, and gasped. There, among the threadbare clothes and the old razor and strop, was the stolen food.

Buck walked over. His eyes widened as he knelt beside me, took the bag of flour, and turned it over and over in his hands. "I can't believe it. He didn't even eat it. Was he trying to starve us? Starve you?"

I looked up into Buck's wide eyes and shook my head. "He never knew anything but fear. He grew skinny shoring up against it. I think he died trying to save himself from it."

"God have mercy." We were both silent for a long moment, remembering Jonah, wondering what might have been if he'd been stronger, if he'd been sane.

"What is that?" Buck gestured toward a silken bundle.

I lifted the small, wrapped object. It was tied with a blue ribbon, the bow giving way easily as I pulled it apart. "I don't . . ." I struggled for breath as the cloth fell away, revealing a photograph. I gazed up at Buck, my lips compressed and quivering.

"It's you."

"Yes."

"He loved you."

"The best he could. Yes."

The photograph had yellowed with age; the young woman staring back at me was thin and pale, strained, and in her eyes, I saw fear. I folded it up and eased it back in its silken ribbons, as if it were made of spiderwebs . . . or snowflakes. He'd been as fragile and yet as intricately designed as a snowflake.

My brother had melted in the heat of life, and there was nothing I could have done about it.

Buck grasped my hand. "Forgive yourself, Ellen. You did the best you could, more than most folks would have. Let him go."

I looked up into his sure eyes. Did he speak the truth? Had I really done the best I could have by Jonah? I could have found a way to keep him alive . . . I should have found a way. "But I failed."

"God did not give you this burden. It was placed on you by your parents—first by your father leaving and then by your mother making you promise to give up your life and future for your brother. That wasn't God, Ellen."

"But God expects us to give up our lives for each other."

"Yes, He does say to lay down our lives for each other. But in His time and way. In seasons. When we obey Him and trust Him to help carry our burdens, it brings life; it doesn't rob it."

I looked down at my hands. I hadn't leaned on God for help or strength. I'd tried to carry the burden of Jonah by myself. If I'd had more faith and trusted God, would things have turned out differently? Grief stabbed at me anew, and for the first time I realized how important it was, how life changing it could be, to trust and obey God.

"Come on." Buck hauled me up and then turned back to packing the empty sled with his supplies.

I bit down on my lower lip as I watched his movements, so familiar from the trail, swift, determined, economical. "When are you leaving?"

"Within the hour." He faced me and pulled out a leather pouch from his coat pocket. "Take this. You'll be stuck here until spring thaw, and I want you to find a decent place to stay."

The fact that he could give me his money but not his heart tore through me like a lance, making me feel no better than a charity case to him. Besides, I would never be able to repay him. "No, I'll be fine. Jonah and I had enough to get us through one winter."

Buck stared hard at me, as if trying to see if I was telling the truth.

"Really. I—I will get a job." I paused. It took every ounce of courage I possessed to ask, but I had to know. "Buck, did you mean it when you promised to be back for Christmas?"

His face held tension and pain. It was as if he were torn in half, having to leave me and yet unable to stay. Sorrow filled his eyes, but compassion was there too—and longing? "Yes, Ellen. I will be back for Christmas."

Joy shot through me. I didn't deserve it, I knew, but I could still hope. "Be careful, okay?" I held out the bundled photograph. "Would you?" I looked up into his eyes and bared my soul to him, risking rejection again. "Would you like to have it?"

Buck considered the photograph for a long moment and then reached for it. With deliberate care he placed it in his coat pocket, where it would lay close to his heart.

I allowed the hope that he would take it out often and remember me reach my eyes.

And then I turned to go.

Chapter Eight

The cold was like an attack—a plaintive, gusting blow against my body. The wind took my breath, and my nose swelled red and pulsing, cheeks stinging from the sharp ice particles in the air as I trudged up Front Street looking for a hotel. Warmth, fire, food, shelter. Comforts that meant so little until they were so far from being gained.

The street was crowded with people wandering up and down the bazaarlike marketplace where stampeders hawked their goods—mostly the one-ton outfit required to enter into Canada. Others shopped and argued prices over a shovel, a pickax, or a prized broom. Some folks looked like they knew where they were going and what they were about, but many others appeared lost and wandering. I identified with the latter group as anxiety gnawed at my stomach. I needed a plan.

The first, most important task was finding a place to stay. I had a little over two hundred dollars in my pocket, and it needed to last until I could find a job, if a job could be found.

I could pray for help and guidance.

The thought surprised me. God hadn't looked down and noticed me or answered my prayers when I'd called out to Him over the years. I'd given up and stopped praying a long time ago. But what if God was there? What if I'd been praying for the wrong solution? What if God had been answering me all along, and I'd just refused to listen? What if He'd had a plan for Jonah and, yes, me, and I'd not been able to accept anything other than what my own two eyes could see and what my ears had heard? What if I'd never really exercised even a mustard seed's worth of faith? I stopped, prickles of truth bright on my skin.

What if God really did love me and care?

I looked up and saw that I was standing in front of the Regina Hotel. Well, it was somewhere to start. I might not have the courage to pray just yet, but God was talking to me, and I intended to try my best to listen. Maybe this was the place.

I stepped inside and stopped short. My goodness, it was a handsome place! My gaze took in the plush blue and cream rugs scattered over the high-polished wood floor where seating groups were arranged for the comfort of the guests. The wallpaper was gold and ivory and practically glittered it was so fine. I walked over to the clerk at the desk and cleared my throat.

"Yes, ma'am. How may I help you?" He was a middle-aged fellow with a long mustache and assessing eyes.

"How much for a room, sir?"

"One hundred and fifty dollars a week."

I gasped. Our last house back in California had cost a hundred dollars for a whole month. The man's mouth dipped down as he noted my reaction.

"Are all the hotels in Dawson so expensive?"

"Most are. You might try the boardinghouses." He turned away as if no longer willing to waste time on me.

I gathered up my pack and slung it onto my shoulder and turned to go.

It was as the man said. After venturing into three more hotels, I had the sinking realization that if I didn't find a job, and soon, I would be in real trouble. Everything in Dawson was at least quadruple the price of what it was back in the States. Maybe I should have taken Buck's money.

I pressed my lips together into a tight line as another realization burned through my mind with searing clarity—a stubborn hardness resided in my heart and it was robbing me of . . . I wasn't exactly sure the full picture of it, but it was huge. I took a deep breath, looking around at the people rushing past me on the busy street. They seemed so sure of themselves while I wasn't sure of anything anymore.

I spent the next three hours looking for a job. There was the Chinese laundry, the dentist office, a drug emporium, a dry goods store, and a bank. I didn't rule out anything. The men were only too willing to talk to me, but the answer at each place was the same: "We regret that we don't need any help."

Desperation and hopelessness weighed heavy on my shoulders as I entered the Big Bear—a restaurant and boardinghouse. It wasn't fair! Here I was doing my best to hear God, and it looked as if He wasn't answering again. I took a deep breath and blew the air out of ballooning cheeks, not that anyone noticed. The dining room was packed with noisy, laughing, talking men crowded around every table, shoveling in heaping spoonfuls of what looked to be stew into their bearded faces.

A harried, plain-faced serving girl stopped next to me long enough to ask, "You be needing a table? There ain't any for just one, but I can squeeze you in with those other ladies." She pointed to a table of four fashionably dressed women.

"Oh no. I'm looking for the owner. Is he terribly busy right now?" The noon rush was probably not the best time to bother him.

"Mrs. Larkin owns this here place." She pointed to a low bench by the door. "Just sit there a minute, and I'll see if I can fetch her. Your name, ma'am?"

"Ellen Pierce."

She nodded and scurried off, her skirt flapping behind her like a sail in the wind. Maybe I would have some luck here. It looked as if they could use the help.

A full twenty minutes later a woman with an enormous bosom and triple chins hurried toward me with a frown in her eyes. I stood and smiled as pleasantly as possible considering my heart was pounding like a trapped rabbit. She looked me up and down, the frown spreading to her down-turned mouth.

"What can I do for you, miss?" Her voice was a sharp staccato.

I clasped my hands tight together in front of my stomach. "I was hoping you might need some help, Mrs. Larkin. I am looking for a job."

Her gaze roved over my face as her eyes narrowed. "I don't need the kind of trouble you would attract."

"Trouble? Oh no, ma'am. I'm a very good worker. And a good cook too."

The woman gave a short, fast shake of her head, and my heart plummeted. "I don't need any help, I said. Now go on."

My hand rose toward her as desperation jerked at my stomach. "I'll work for room and board."

Mrs. Larkin took a firm grasp on my forearm, the vein in her forehead growing larger and blue. She jerked me toward the door and pushed me out, slamming the door in my face without another word.

I stumbled onto the walkway, arms out for balance, but it didn't help. I crashed onto my side with a groan as my shoulder hit the hard-packed snowdrift. Tears stung my eyes. I slowly sat up and blinked against the cold, bright outdoors.

I guess You're not going to answer my prayers now either.

I wanted to stay there and give in to the feeling of hopelessness and have a good cry, but I couldn't. I took a deep breath and struggled to stand, trying to ignore the throbbing pain in my shoulder, and turned toward Front Street. I didn't really see where I was going or notice that the crowd was thicker and livelier. I barely noticed the grand hotels, hastily thrown up shacklike shops, saloons, and hundreds of tents. I just wandered, aimless and numb.

"Ellen? Ellen is that you?"

I turned to see Kate leaning from the half-open door of the—I glanced at the big sign above her head—*Monte Carlo Saloon and Dance Hall.* She waved me over, laughing. "Come inside and get warmed up. You look frozen through!"

The fact that I should continue searching for a job and a place to stay battled with the very real grumbling of my stomach and the frozen tingling in my feet and face. "I shouldn't go in a place like that."

"Oh, posh! This is Dawson, Ellen. None of that kind of propriety stands to reason out here. Now come inside before you turn into an icicle. I'll get you some breakfast." Her smile was dazzling.

"Well, just for a few minutes to warm up." I looked around and saw that, indeed, no one seemed to care in the least that I was stepping into a saloon.

Kate led me over to a round table and pulled out a chair. "Just sit a spell while I round up something hot for you to eat."

I nodded, taking in the patrons and the décor. A long bar occupied one end with a smoky, wavy mirror hanging on the wall behind it. The room was well lit from the many windows and several chandeliers burning, even though it was early in the day. The walls had flocked velvet green and purple wall coverings on them, and the floor was high-polished wood planks.

More than a dozen people sat at the tables around me. Four men were playing cards at the table I faced. A young man plucked a cheerful song from the piano, and two young women, expensively dressed and perfectly coifed, hugged the end of the bar, chatting with each other. It didn't seem as bad as I imagined it would be. It actually seemed pretty nice.

Sighing at my assessment, I slumped back in the chair and worked off my mittens. My goodness, how the cold had taken grip of my hands!

"Here you go, dear." Kate set a plate of eggs, bacon, and a biscuit in front of me along with a steaming cup of coffee. My mouth watered as the smells drifted to my nose. "So, have you found a place to stay?" Kate sat across from me and folded her elegant hands on top of the table.

I paused, shook my head, and took a bite of bacon. "Everything is so expensive. I didn't realize the costs here were so much greater. My couple of hundred dollars is not going to last long."

"Yes, not many realize that when they finally land here. You'll need to find a job quick." She raised her brows in silent question.

"Don't even consider it." My tone lowered to a hushed hiss. "I'll never be a prostitute."

"Of course not," Kate snapped back. "If you hadn't rushed off . . . if you would have let me explain, you might be surprised by my offer."

I eyed her with raised brows and dove into my eggs. I'd heard eggs were two dollars each, and I wasn't about to let them grow cold.

Kate motioned a hand around the room. "The Monte Carlo is one of my dancing halls. A dancing hall is a respectable place, Ellen. The women I employ"—she gestured with her head toward the two women at the end of the bar—"get paid to dance with the men, a waltz or a square dance, that's all, nothing more."

I glanced at the young women in question. One was blonde, plump, and pretty. The other was dark with big slanting eyes and striking facial features.

"They charge a dollar a dance, which they split with the house at the end of each night. On a busy night those girls have made over two hundred dollars."

I sputtered, choking on my coffee. That was more money than Jonah or I had been able to make in a month.

Kate clicked her fingernails on the table and leaned in. "As pretty as you are, you would make a fortune. There's more ways to strike it rich out here than slopping around in icy streambeds and panning for gold, you know." She sat back and smiled, her perfect pink lips pressed together in satisfaction.

"Kate, I appreciate the offer, but I couldn't. I don't know anything about men, normal men anyway. I just couldn't."

She looked down at her hands. "I understand, Ellen, more than you know." She looked up at me with eyes that had gone from smug to vulnerable.

I put down my fork. "How did you end up being a . . . a prostitute?"

Kate shrugged a slim shoulder. "It didn't start out that way. I came here near the beginning of the rush, with my husband."

"Oh, I'm sorry. Did he die?"

"Don't be sorry. He was a meal ticket out of small-town life. A traveling salesman. He died on the rapids, and I can't honestly say I missed him. I arrived in Dawson with five dollars to my name, a one-ton outfit, and my husband's wares. That was a bit of luck, I'll tell you." She grinned.

"I thought him a fool to bring brooms to this frozen tundra to sell, but no one had thought of that. I made my grubstake on wooden handles and straw." Her laugh tinkled through the room. "But I didn't buy a claim, no." She lifted a hand. "I bought my first saloon. It wasn't long before women started coming in, and I saw an opportunity. The men here are lonely, Ellen, and they were getting rich fast with nothing to spend it on. I found the need and supplied it with dance-hall girls."

"Not prostitutes?"

"Not at first. After a time I noticed some of the girls were making their own deals with men after their shift here. It was a dirty business, like the fallen birds on Paradise Alley. I knew I could do better so I built a fancy brothel, hired the prettiest women I could find, and charged through the roof for their services. A year later I owned several businesses with the gold dust flowing like a fast-moving stream right into my pockets."

"But what about you? Did you . . . ?"

"I didn't need to. I was busy running the places and didn't need the money."

"But I saw you, that night, with—"

Kate's mouth flattened in a hard line, but her eyes spoke the sorrow of a wounded heart. "I met a man, my first and only love." She smiled in a self-deprecating way. "A gambler, of course. He was one tall, dark, and handsome drink of water, and I fell hard. I gave him everything—my heart, my body, my soul. He promised to marry me."

"He didn't?"

"Left me standing at the altar like a desperate fool and skulked out of town. I hope he's dead."

"Kate! You can't mean that."

"Well, maybe not dead but suffering. I hope he's suffering real bad." She shrugged a pearl-white shoulder. "After he left, I didn't much care about anything. Something kind of snapped inside me. Here I had all the money and adventure I ever wanted, but it meant nothing to me anymore. One night a man offered me five hundred dollars to share his hotel room. I did it. Not because I wanted the money; I could have gotten more. But because I was lonely and tired of sleeping by myself at night. I'm picky now, but there was a time I would spend the night with anyone decent, just to have him hold me afterward. That was my only demand."

Kate stopped her story, looked down at her clasped hands on the table, and then suddenlike, rallied herself and stared into my eyes. "Sounds pretty pathetic, doesn't it?"

I shook my head. It sounded . . . familiar.

"I know I put on an air of independence; heck, we all do around here. But there is one disease in Dawson City, Ellen, and it infects almost everyone."

"What's that?"

"Its name is loneliness."

Her words, her story, left me breathless. Tears threatened my vision. I knew loneliness too. I knew it so well.

I sat speechless and thinking. Maybe there was no harm in dancing and filling a miner's heart with company for a moment in time. Maybe, as different as I could imagine it, this was God's answer. Maybe God didn't see things at all like I did. I still couldn't quite pray, but my heart was stretching, reaching out to hear Him give me direction, answers.

Kate remained quiet, letting me think. "I owe you an apology, Kate."

"Now, how do you figure that?" The surprise in her eyes was real.

"I judged you. I thought myself better than you, and while I don't think the way you've gone about filling up your loneliness is the right way, I'm sorry how I rejected you for it. You're a good woman, Kate. I mean that."

She blinked rapidly and lifted her chin. "I don't know as anyone has ever said that to me before."

I reached over and placed my hand over the top of hers, grinning to lighten the mood. "God loves you, Kate. He loves both of us, and I'm starting to believe He is the only real answer to anyone's loneliness."

Kate huffed. "You're not going to go and turn all religious on me, are you?"

I laughed. "I just might." I sat back in my chair and studied her guarded face. "Do you think you could get your hands on a Bible?"

Kate smirked. "I can get anything I want, Ellen."

"Well, how about a deal of sorts. I'll be one of your dance-hall girls, and a few times a week we'll read the Bible together."

Kate pursed her lips into a pout and narrowed her eyes. "What makes you think you are in any position to make deals?"

I laughed again. "You've said over and over how much you want me to work for you. Come on, Kate, what are you afraid of?"

"I'm not afraid."

"Well then, how does this being a dance-hall girl work?"

She sighed but I knew she'd given in. "There are rooms upstairs that the girls share—two to a room—and they're real nice. I charge my girls one hundred dollars a month for rent, and that includes two meals a day. Really, you'll not find a better offer in the entire city, I promise you."

"There *is* one other problem."

"Oh?"

"I don't know how to dance."

Her eyes widened, and then she burst out with that tinkling laughter of hers. "I'll teach you myself. I've put on a few pounds of late and could use the exercise."

I glanced at her tiny waist and doubted it. "Kate, I have to ask. Why do you want to help me so badly? I'm used to taking care of others, not someone looking out for me. I don't quite trust it. Tell me the truth."

Kate studied my eyes for a moment. "I'm a business-woman, and you will be good for business. At least that's how it started. Now?" Her brows raised and she leaned in. "There's something special about you, Ellen. I don't know exactly what it is, but I see it. I want us to be friends."

Her gaze turned vulnerable again, hopeful. How could I deny her? She was like the family, the sister, I'd never had.

I popped the last bite of biscuit in my mouth and smiled at her. "Well, being your friend does have its perks."

She rolled her eyes at me but joined in the laughter. I had a feeling I was going to like having a friend very much.

Chapter Nine

uck, what are you doing?

Buck jerked awake and grasped quick hold of the team's reins that were slipping from his cold-locked hands. He shook his head and slapped his thighs with either hand trying to bring some feeling back into his legs. He should jump off the sled and run awhile but . . . had someone spoken to him?

Fully awake now, he looked around at the snow-covered forest land and the river, Forty Mile River, he had been following all day. The landscape of white and black whizzed by, his dog team doing a manful job breaking the trail. Seeing nothing but the great timbered land of pine and rock and a pure blue sky left him feeling a certain amount of warm-faced chagrin that he'd allowed himself to drift off and thought he was hearing voices. But even as he tried to shrug it off, the question remained, echoing around the empty places within his chest.

What *was* he doing?

Lord, You know I won't do anything stupid. A vision of the gun strapped to his hip appeared, fully formed, in his mind's eye. *I just want to hear the story from his own mouth. Then I'd like to haul his yellow-bellied hide into the Northwest Mounted Police and see some justice done. I have to know if it was truly an accident. But if it was carelessness and not giving a whit about anyone but himself . . . Well, then I plan to see that the man rethinks his selfishness and gets a glimpse of what he has done. Someone has to see what it's cost me, Lord.*

Buck paused for a long breath, and the question repeated itself, louder than before, louder than the jangling of the harnesses, louder than the wind song, louder than the rushing of the river beside him.

Son, what are you really doing?

Okay, he was hearing voices. *The* Voice. *Lord, I really have my mind made up about this.*

Ellen's face rushed to the fore of his imagination, squeezing his heart. It wasn't right—how much he missed her, how often he thought of her, how he took her picture out and memorized each curve of her face. The memory of their kiss flowed like liquid heat through his veins. But he couldn't stop. He couldn't go forward until he'd gone back.

He just couldn't.

The town of Forty Mile came into view, causing a rush of mixed emotions to overcome conscious thought. He'd made it. And the man was close; he could feel it.

"Get, Shelby! Get, boys!" Buck gave the reins a gentle slap and set his teeth, ignoring the questions in his heart.

"Ellen, look! A package came for you!"

My roommate, Stella Silverman, better known as Silver Sal, burst through the door of our room with wide blue eyes and a huge smile.

I turned toward her as she thrust two long boxes into my hands. Surprise and excitement filled me, making me laugh at Stella's exuberance. Who could have sent me gifts? Could they be from Buck?

"You must have an admirer already!" Stella teased. "Why you haven't even begun dancing yet. It's not fair at all."

I sat the brown paper-wrapped packages on my bed. "I haven't an admirer. I haven't even met anyone except for a few of the girls."

"Oh, pish-posh, just open it!" Stella squeezed her hands together under her chin, her eyes alight with excitement. Her anticipation was catching, and I picked up the first box. I was pleased that my roommate was proving so friendly. Some of the other girls I'd met had not been quite as welcoming.

As I pulled on one end of the bow, the twine that held the paper down slid free. I paused, my hands splayed in the air above the box, then dove in and peeled back the paper and lifted the lid. I gasped and Stella squealed as I pulled out a silvery blue satin gown. I held it up, marveling at the rich feel of the fabric.

"Oh, I've never seen anything like it. It's so . . . it's so—"

"Conservative?" I finished for her. I would have to thank whoever sent it for being so thoughtful as to give me such a demure dress compared with what I'd seen the other girls wear.

"It's very pretty." Stella laughed. "Oh, wait! Open the next one. And isn't there a card?"

I laid the dress on the bed and dug into the box looking for answers. There, on the bottom, was a slim folded note. I flipped it open and scanned the message as my heart continued to pound loud in my chest.

Dearest Ellen,

This dress is a gift in congratulations of completing your dancing lessons. You are turning out just as I knew you would and are a superb dancer. I would like you to make your debut tonight. The next dress is on credit as you will need at least two to begin your week. I will give you plenty of time to pay it off, but I have the feeling you won't need it. Please be ready by 9:00 p.m. as I shall introduce you myself!

Best of luck,
Kate
P.S. Don't forget to come up with a name!

"You look pale, Ellen. What does the note say? Who is it from?"

My hands shook as I set the note on the bed. Was I really going to do this? "They're from Kate. One is a gift, and the other I'll have to pay for as I can. She wants me to start tonight."

"Heavens to Betsy but she favors you. She's never spent so much time with anyone or given the other girls dresses that I know of. Why is that?" Stella sounded truly jealous for the first time.

I groaned. "It's a bribe, Stella. She thinks I'm going to make her a pot load of money and knows I had reservations about taking this job."

"She's right, you know. You are the prettiest of all the girls by far, and you have an air about you that will attract men like bees to honey."

I looked at her with my brows raised. "That's silly, Stella. You don't know what you're saying."

"Oh yes, I do. I don't know exactly how to explain it, but I know men, and they will want to figure out your mystery." She flashed a grin at me. "Just wait and see. You're going to be wonderful! Now let's see the other dress."

I couldn't believe I had hoped the packages were from Buck. He probably hadn't even thought of me, not like I was thinking about him anyway—daily, hourly. I took a deep breath and complied.

Stella gulped and then oohed and aahed as I pulled forth a pile of pink froth. The gown was complete with ruffles and rich black ribbons. It had long ballooning sleeves, and I couldn't help but think it was pretty.

"Oh, Ellen. Try them on! Which one will you wear tonight?"

I supposed I should wear the first one since it was Kate's gift. "I guess, I should try them on."

It was strange sharing a room with another woman. All my life I'd had my own bedroom and the privacy that lent me. Stella thought nothing about stripping naked in front of me—she'd had sisters, lots of them—but I was mortified by the idea of anyone seeing me in my undergarments and turned away from her gleeful eyes. She rushed over to work the buttons up the back of the silver-blue gown and helped me tie the velvet silver ribbon at the back. It was a perfect fit.

I turned around, my fingers fluttering around the skirt. I looked down at the rows of gathered folds on the skirt, the sound of the material swishing as a turned. I'd *never* had a dress like this.

"It's perfect." Stella smiled, her dimples flashing in her round cheeks, blonde hair bobbing. "Well, don't just stand there! Go look in the glass!"

A long mirror on a swiveled hinge that could be adjusted to see all sides stood in the corner of our room. I walked over toward it and stared at the figure in the glass.

"It's no wonder they call Kate Queen of Dawson," Stella murmured with awe. "She's a genius. It couldn't be more perfect for you."

I hated to admit it, but Stella was right. Kate couldn't have found a better way to introduce her newest dancing girl to the miners of Dawson City.

And that girl was me.

The steps that took me to the ground floor of the Monte Carlo were narrow, the tips of my pointy slippers hanging over their edge, as the steps creaked in protest, like my heart. My silver blue gown whispered around my legs as

I descended down, down, down into a world I had never seen or imagined.

Jonah had always kept us alone. Quiet. My life was silent with bursts of fright or anger. Red outbursts against the haze of gray. Now, as I walked down those steps, Kate's beautiful, glorious face beckoned me with her eyes toward this new life.

The piano was in full swing. I'd met Ragtime Kid once before . . . ran into him in a hall in the morning hours while we were both passing with breakfast on our plates. He usually played at the Dominion Saloon and was well known there, but Kate had handed him a heavy purse for my debut. I had learned that and other ripe gossip after trying on my gowns. The girls of the house had flooded in to see what the fuss was about, envy riding high in their arched brows and pursed lips. Everyone, it seemed, knew how much trouble Kate had put into me . . . my coming out.

I clutched the railing that slid beneath my elbow-length, white-gloved hand and pressed back the knot in my stomach. I reached the bottom step and paused; Kate grasped my upper arm in a tender-tight hold. I looked up at her as the music ground to a crushing, weighty halt. All eyes turned. All those faces. All those men.

I let my gaze wander from eye to eye to eye. I breathed in tiny breaths.

"Don't be shy." Kate's voice was a small, almost silent whisper in my head and in my heart. "They are going to love you."

Love me? No one loved me. They might need me, use me as a balm to cover heart holes and mind fears, but love *me?* Only one man had ever made me feel loved, and I'd practically stolen those moments. *Oh, Buck.*

A little sob escaped my painted red lips. I started to press my white-gloved hand against them and then remembered the stain that mistake would cause. I lowered my hand back to my side and let Kate lead me farther into the lantern-lit room.

I could hear my breath go in and out. Kate took my hand, held it high, like a prize, and turned me in a slow circle, round and round, as if we were dancing some strange dance she was master of. She stopped in a sudden way that made me almost stumble, and then she held our clasped hands high in the air.

"Gentlemen! Gentlemen." Her voice lowered to a soft purr that held every man in taut silence. They craned forward to hear her words, as if an angel stood among them.

"Gentlemen, I give you—" She smiled down at me, whispering, "Have you thought of a name, dear?"

I shook my head, my eyes filling with tears that I blinked and blinked back until they were hidden in my heart.

She shrugged a silken shoulder and turned back to her rapt audience. "I give you the golden girl of your dreams. I give you the gemstone of Dawson City. Gentlemen . . . I give you Jewel."

Chapter Ten

The line to dance with me formed immediately with cheering. I gulped down my fear, hoping I would remember the steps to the waltz, polka, schottische, and square dance. I was told that on most nights, the dance hall boasted a play or vaudeville acts before the dancing began. Many dancing girls were also actresses in plays ranging from *East Lynne* to *Camille*. I shuddered at the thought of being on stage, the center of every eye and ear, but had the feeling of being swept along on a tide where I had no foothold.

149

The first man was tall and thin. He had a wiry mustache and an easy smile. I took a deep breath and let him pull me onto the floor. The music of a four-instrument orchestra sprang to life—piano, violin, trombone, and cornet. The music of a waltz swept over me, and I loved it. I never had many opportunities to listen to music. We didn't attend church, and I was rarely invited to socials where music was played or sung. A whole new room had opened in my heart with this music.

My instructions were clear. My job was to dance around the perimeter of the room with the other couples until the music stopped, an abrupt freezing of the dance floor like in the game musical chairs. And then I would lead my current partner to the bar while I took the hand of the next and the next. The long hours of the night twirled and whirled from my feet and heated face. I couldn't help it. Kate was right once again. I loved dancing.

"You sure are a pretty one. Where'd Queenie find you?"

Queenie was Kate's nickname as all the girls, both the dancing girls and the prostitutes on Paradise Alley, had taken one. "I came from California, looking for gold."

The man chuckled, his teeth soured with chewing tobacco. I wanted to feel disgust, but I didn't. I looked into his eyes and saw a vulnerability I had lost long ago and a good heart.

Sorrow gripped my heart for him as I stared into his eyes. "Where are you from?"

His eyes lit up by my interest. "All the way from Mississippi, ma'am."

"That's a long way. Did you leave family there?"

He nodded as we spun around the room. "Three brothers and a mother. She's doin' poorly so I thought I would strike out into the world. Find my fortune for us all."

"And have you found it, sir?"

He looked over my shoulder at the other whirling dancers and shook his head with an exhaled huff and a half grin. "I did this night."

I blushed, the heat of jolted embarrassment filling my cheeks more than the excursion of the dance. A choice leapt within my mind. I could be coy. I could flirt. I could bat my lashes and giggle like the other girls. But all I wanted to do was take his sweet, tired soul into my arms and comfort him like a mother.

Oh, Lord! If I am in this much sympathetic turmoil on my first night, what will I be like by the end of the week? Give me something to say to him. Give me some of Your hope and vision for this man.

I'd prayed! I actually cried out to God for the first time in longer than I could remember. "What's your name?"

"Joel Hobson, ma'am."

An idea formed as fast as I spoke it. "Well, Joel Hobson, I'm taking down names tonight for those who want prayer. Would you like to be on my list?"

"You're a religious woman?" His brows shot up to his receding hairline.

"I love God . . . and I pray. I'd like to pray for those who want it."

The music ground to a sudden halt. We swayed with the effort to still ourselves. I allowed him to take my arm and then steered him toward the bar as instructed. Just before releasing his grasp on me, he leaned in and whispered in my ear, "You surely are a jewel. I'd like to be on that list."

I bit my lower lip and nodded. What had I done? One prayer didn't make me any kind of expert. I didn't have my own life figured out, so how were my prayers going to help anyone else? The joy faded as doubt raised its ugly head and stared me straight in the eyes.

Dear Buck,

I heard you were in Forty Mile, and while I know you may never receive this letter, I wanted to write out my thoughts to you. I'm staying at the El Dorado Saloon and Dancing Hall and have taken a job as one of the queen of Dawson's famed dancing girls. You might be surprised by this news, and then again, when I think of all you have been through in your life, all that you've seen, I think you might understand.

Most of the men are a decent sort. They want someone to talk to, someone to listen and care. A few are frightening to me. When I am asked to dance with a man who has that lustful stare, looking me up and down in a way that makes my spine crawl, then I question my decisions. But I've found something, some key. I didn't realize the lesson of it when Jonah was alive, but in living with him, I learned a talent. I learned how to look beyond a face and see into a hurting, lonely soul. I have begun to pray again, for others at least. I pray for you every day. If anyone deserves God's grace, it is you.

I miss your face. I miss your crystal eyes that glow like blue ice. I miss your strong voice and shoulder and the curve of your neck. I miss your kisses. I miss you.

You promised to come back for Christmas. I cross off each day and wonder, will you come? Even if you have not healed your heart by confronting your past, will you come? Even though you promised me, and promises broken are all I've known, will you come?

Regardless. You will live forever in my heart.
Ellen

I stared at the letter, my hands trembling, and tried to keep the dripping tears from staining the yet-dry ink. Should I really post it? My heart galloped at the thought of him reading my deepest, innermost thoughts.

My body answered my question before my mind and will had thought it out and made a conscious decision. I rose from the bed, sealed the letter, and wrote out the address. I walked from the room with strong, determined steps, into the parlor, dim and empty, and laid the letter on the table by the door where all letters to be posted were laid.

I placed my letter, my heart, on top of the small pile and backed away. Then I covered my face and cried.

Chapter Eleven

welve days until Christmas.

Stella and I squeezed in with the hundreds of people attending Father Judge's Sunday service. The crowd grew quiet and respectful as he entered from a side door. Surprise filled me at his appearance. The man's clothes hung in tatters around his elbows and ankles, looking more like rags than anything else.

His face spoke of wrinkled exhaustion, but then he turned and scanned the crowd, his gaze locking with mine for a few seconds. I inhaled—a sharp, sudden breath. His eyes held a light that beamed with an almost supernatural intensity of pure love. And when he began to speak, his thin voice quivered with adoration for God.

We all sat or stood, elbow to elbow, motionless to catch every word.

The words he read from Psalm 139 caught in my heart, and I repeated them over and over in my mind to memorize them:

> "For thou hast covered me in my mother's womb. I will praise thee; for I am fearfully and wonderfully made: marvelous are thy works; and that my soul knoweth right well. . . . When I was made in secret, and curiously wrought in the lowest parts of the earth. Thine eyes did see my substance, yet being unperfect. . . . How precious also are thy thoughts unto me, O God! how great is the sum of them! If I should count them, they are more in number than the sand: when I awake, I am still with thee."

The picture the words painted of God making me and knowing me that intimately . . . Did He really have so many thoughts toward me? Did that kind of love really exist? That it might robbed me of breath and then filled me with warmth. I wanted to believe it, but the facts of my life made it look untrue. My muscles strained with the questions.

Oh, Buck, I wish you were here so I could talk to you.

After the service Stella leaned toward my ear. "He's called the saint of Dawson, you know. He started a hospital when Dawson was just a tent city, and it's nursed many a soul back to health."

I nodded, knowing the priest's reputation as a selfless servant to the community. Maybe, if I could get close to him, Father Judge would talk to me. "I heard they are asking for volunteers since the nuns didn't arrive to nurse the patients. Do you think they would let me volunteer?"

"Of course he would. I just can't believe you aren't as tuckered out as the rest of us by Sunday." Stella clutched my arm as we jostled our way through the departing crowd and out onto the street.

I raised my eyebrows at her. "As if you nap all day. Will you be going to visit Tom this afternoon?"

She giggled, looking pleased with herself. "He is my beau, you know. Why, with him being a bartender at the Tivoli and me dancing all night, I hardly ever get to see him."

I'd heard about the infamous Tom Baker. He was rumored to be one of the miners' favorite bartenders— telling hilarious stories, giving advice, and weighing the gold dust in the miners' favor more often than not. Stella had filled in his physical description saying he was dark haired with a long mustache and goatee, golden green eyes, and a smile that melted her heart.

"Well, have a nice afternoon, Stella."

"Oh, I will. You have a good time with all those sick people." She wrinkled her nose and waved good-bye. I couldn't help but smile at the wink she gave me before she turned and sauntered down the busy street with a cheerful gait.

As I made my way through the throngs of townsfolk, a nervous rumbling turned in my stomach. What if Father Judge rejected me? What if dance-hall girls were considered little better than the prostitutes on Paradise Alley and not allowed entrance to the town's better establishments?

Names like Nellie the Pig, Oregon Mare, and Goldtooth Gert, who really did have a gold tooth, sprang to mind. What if they only knew me as Jewel? It wasn't as if I had any great nursing skills with which to boast.

I tried my best to squash such thoughts as I entered the large two-story log building that was Saint Mary's Hospital. It was quiet in the small reception area. I took off my bonnet and let it dangle by the silk ribbons from my hand as I wandered farther inside.

I walked up to a faded painting of Mary holding the baby Jesus and stared at it. The artist had captured the love shining out of a mother's eyes for her child. What would it be like to have a child of my own? The realization that I'd never considered it before jolted me. Had the weight of Jonah's care robbed me of a young woman's desire to have a family? I wasn't sure I had the courage to be a mother. What if I turned out like my father and abandoned my child?

"May I be of service?" a gentle voice asked.

I jerked at the sound, so deep were my thoughts, and turned. Father Judge seemed even smaller in person, frail as a much older man would be, with small, sunken eyes behind round glasses, a gaunt face, and dark, receding hair. "I—I would like to volunteer my services, that is, help with the sick on Sunday afternoons, if you could use the help."

The man took in my fancy dress, and for a moment shame filled me. I wasn't good enough for this place. "I have a little nursing experience," I rushed out.

A smile and the glow I had seen earlier lit his face. "We would welcome your help, Miss . . . ?"

"Oh." I breathed a sigh and walked forward to shake his hand. "Ellen Pierce."

"So good of you to come, child. Here, let me show you around."

The two front rooms were a receiving room and the priest's office. Two examination rooms were in the middle of the first floor along with a kitchen and small bedroom with only a cot and washstand against the back wall. Upstairs was a long, open room, running the entire length of the building, filled with rows of cots. Several men lay on them, and they cheered up, talking and waving at us as Father Judge walked into the room.

The priest stopped by every bed, fluffed a pillow or two, tousled the hair of men hardly younger than he as if they were boys, and joked with the patients. The look of joy and love on their faces took my breath. It was clear they adored him.

After checking on each patient, with me trailing after him, Father Judge stopped and introduced me to the room at large. The men let out a cheer, heating my cheeks.

"Isn't that Jewel? From the Monte Carlo?" someone from behind me asked.

My gaze shot to the priest's and froze. "He speaks the truth. I guess I should have told you that." I hesitated, looking around at the men. "Do you still want me to help?"

"Of course we do. Not one of us is greater than another in God's eyes."

I inhaled suddenly as the thought registered. "What can I do?"

"I think for today you should learn our schedule. The men have already had their noon meal, but I have a feeling you have not?"

"Oh, but I'm not hungry. You can put me right to work."

The older man stared long into my eyes, and peace flowed from him. I had to push back tears. *Get a hold of yourself, Ellen.*

"Very well, then. Could you write some letters for the patients? Many of them haven't the strength to hold a pen."

I thought of all the letters I had been writing to Buck. Yes, letters I could do.

Within ten minutes the priest set me up with the necessary writing implements and a wooden stool to scoot from bed to bed. The hours passed like fleeting clouds scudding across the sky. And like clouds I saw pictures of each man's life as he wrote to his loved ones back home. I smiled at the end of the day. My heart was now well and truly turned toward these patients, and my desire to help them in any way had become a burning hope as I heard their stories of home.

Father Judge could not have given me a better first task, and I was almost certain he knew it.

It was late and the hospital quiet as I pulled on my coat. I peeked in the tiny office looking for Father Judge to say good night. He was reading a worn-looking book I assumed was a Bible, but he looked up and gave me a gentle smile, then motioned toward the chair. "Ellen, please come in a moment. I want to thank you."

I took a step inside. "There is no need to thank me. It was a pleasure to help."

"Oh, but I must. As you can see, few people are willing to give up their Sunday for others. It is a rare quality you have."

I shrugged, not knowing what to say to such praise.

"Have you always served others?"

"I suppose so. My family needed me. I took care of my brother for the last several years, but he . . . he died and now I don't know what to do."

"I see."

The way he said it made me think he saw something I didn't. "What do you see?"

"I see a lovely young woman trying to find her purpose in life."

I sat on the chair and sighed. "Yes, with my old purpose gone, I don't know what to do."

"Do you know what you want?"

Buck's face flashed through my mind. I blushed and looked down.

Father Judge laughed. "You have an idea?"

"I want a family—my own family," I whispered.

"God places desires in our hearts, child. There is nothing to be ashamed about."

"I'm afraid."

"What do you fear?"

"He won't love me back. He'll never be able to."

"Ah." Father Judge closed his eyes and bowed his head. I remained quiet while he silently prayed. When he looked back up, he smiled at me, and a rush of peace flowed from his eyes to my heart. "I will pray for you every day that

God will grant you the desires of your heart. Be at peace, Ellen."

I stood with tears clouding my vision. No one had ever prayed for me that I knew of, and certainly not daily. First Kate and now Father Judge. Why was it that Dawson, a city so far away from anywhere, had people in it who cared for me? "Thank you, Father."

He stood, came around the worn desk, and gave my hand a squeeze. "Go in peace, child."

"I'll see you next Sunday."

"Even if you don't come back, even if you stop serving others, God still loves you, and I will still pray for you. You don't have to earn it, you know."

It was another new thought. Why did I feel like I didn't deserve love?

I left the hospital full of questions, but the feeling of God's peace remained all through the night.

Chapter Twelve

"So, how many marriage proposals did you get tonight, Ellen?"

It was four o'clock in the morning, and Kate sat across from me at a table in the emptying dance hall. I laughed. "Only two tonight. One of them claimed to have dug out two hundred thousand dollars' worth of gold from his claim."

Kate's mouth kicked up in a sideways smile. "Well, goodness gracious, girl. Why didn't you take him up on his offer? That sounds like a real catch to me."

I sipped the hot coffee and let my face go blank and serious. "The top of his head came to my nose, and he had two missing teeth among the rotten ones. I'm holding out for a little better."

Kate threw back her head and laughed. I smiled at her.

Kate had held up her end of the bargain. She stopped by every couple of days to check on the business, and she always made time to sit and chat with me and listened while I read the Bible. Her observations and comments about what we read revealed her wit and intelligence and often shocked me or made me laugh. There was nothing she was afraid to say, and I found myself thinking about the people in the Bible in a new way. Aside from Father Judge, Kate was the most honest person I'd ever known.

One of her elegant eyebrows arched, and I knew she was about to be very honest.

"I don't suppose any man around here could catch your heart. It's already taken, isn't it?" A look of compassionate knowing emanated from her eyes.

"I suppose it is." My voice was soft in agreement as I took another sip and hid part of my face with the cup.

Kate sat up, her face alight with mischief. "I have an idea that will take your mind off him."

I rolled my eyes and set down the cup. This was not going to be good.

"Christmas is just four days away, right?"

I nodded, my stomach clenching at the reminder. Would Buck really come?

"I'm thinking of having an auction."

I blinked once. "What kind of auction?"

She tilted her head sideways and flashed white teeth at me. "Why a 'Bride for Christmas' auction, of course."

I groaned. It was worse than I thought. "That's a terrible idea."

Her lips pursed in a pretend pout. "It's a wonderful idea and you know it. The men are never lonelier than on Christmas day. You girls will fetch a small fortune, and I will split it with you fifty/fifty."

"Kate . . . if you use the word *wife*, you know they will want a wife, with all the wifely duties included. You need to take this idea to Paradise Alley."

"Those men can have the fallen birds on that street any time they want. Now listen. I will make it clear on the advertisements that it is not a real marriage with bedroom expectations. Just spend the day with a lonely man, cook him a nice Christmas dinner, listen to his stories, and pretend to care about him for twenty-four hours. It's brilliant!"

If the men abided by such rules, and after getting to know many of them I thought they would, I had to admit she would make a small fortune in one evening. But it was still risky. The girls would have to go home with the miner and no longer be under the protection of the Monte Carlo.

"It might be brilliant, but I'm not interested." I couldn't tell her that Buck might, just might, come back for Christmas, and I couldn't be pretending to be somebody's wife if he walked through the door. I couldn't tell her that, but the light in her eyes told me I didn't have to.

"I'll make you a deal."

I sat back in my chair and crossed my arms over my chest, waiting.

"If you participate, I will personally pay off the remaining debt for Saint Mary's Hospital." Her lips curved up as her eyes slanted. "I know how much you love that place."

I didn't know whether to laugh or strangle her. The hospital had substantial debt, and the possibility of clearing it . . . the look on Father Judge's face when he was told? I pressed my lips together in a tight line and glared at Kate.

She had the good sense not to gloat.

If Buck did come back, I could always explain. He would understand if it was for a good cause, wouldn't he?

"You always get what you want, don't you, Kate?" The resentment in my voice was as thick as molasses.

She shrugged, a look of determination filling her eyes. "I always want good things, Ellen. Everyone wins—the miners, you girls, me, and most of all, the hospital. What's so wrong with that?"

I sighed. "All right, Kate. You win . . . again. When is the auction?"

"Christmas Eve, of course. Right here in the dance hall." Her eyes fairly twinkled with excitement. "And tonight we will spread the word and hint, a planted rumor if you will, that Dawson's own Jewel will be on the auction block."

The nightmare washed back over me like cold fingers clawing at my back. I sat up, a sudden gasping of breath, and slowly blinked awake. It was an old dream, one I hadn't had in years, but as chilling as the first time.

I swung my feet to the floor and stood up to pace. My breath made puffs of vapor in the freezing air, but my shivering was from more than the cold. I saw it again— my father with big chains in his hands, wrapping them around my mother's throat. He tightened the chains, slowly cutting off her breath, until she sagged against the back of the chair.

It was just a dream. Just a dream.

I repeated the phrase until my heartbeat slowed, but I couldn't shake off the crawling sensation on my back. *Oh, Buck. I wish you were here. I wish I had someone to talk to. I wish I had someone to hold me. I'm so tired of being alone.*

I sat back on the bed and pulled the blanket around me, trying to be quiet and not wake Stella. The early morning light filtered in through the cracks of the dark curtains as I laid my forehead against my upraised knees.

Dear Lord, why did my father have to leave? Why wasn't he strong enough? I need someone to talk to. I've been praying for everyone else—the men, Kate, the girls here, Buck—but I am afraid to pray for myself. I'm afraid You won't be there for me either, just like my father . . .

Tears trickled from beneath my tightly closed eyes as I said the truth in my heart. Why did I think God might answer my prayers for others but not for me?

The dream washed back over me, and I saw my father's face. It turned from loving affection to snarling, lip-curling hatred directed at my mother. He had hated her. Hated what she put him through with her emotional and physical problems, and that's why he left. It wasn't my fault. I hadn't done anything wrong. I'd picked up his place when he left and kept everything and everyone together the best I could. And Jonah? Jonah had demanded we come here. I had tried to take the very best care of him that I could. I took a long, shaky breath. It wasn't my fault that he died.

Lord, show me what You think of me. Those Scriptures said You have thoughts toward me, outnumbering the sand. Tell me Your thoughts.

Nothing came for a long time, and then flashes of light flickered behind my closed eyes. I saw myself in a glowing white gown lying in a grassy meadow with wildflowers of every color swaying in a sweet-smelling breeze all around me. Upon my head was a crown of entwined wildflowers and bright green leaves. My feet were bare and my hands were outstretched. The breeze blew over me and somehow through me from my feet, up and up, to my head bringing with it a deep and profound sense of peace. A small smile played across my lips as I simply rested.

Gone was all the fear, all the anxiety about the future, all the struggles of wants and desires unfulfilled. The peace was so strong, so alive, there wasn't room for anything else. Like a bright light, it conquered every inch of my darkness. I laughed.

It started as a small giggle and then built and built until I threw myself back on the bed in a fit of pure joy. I laughed until tears poured down my cheeks as the relief of knowing God's peace and care for me spread through my core to touch and tingle every part of my body.

God hadn't left me at all! I'd just forgotten He was there.

"Ellen! Whatever is the matter with you?"

I turned over to see Stella standing over me with wide, panicked eyes. Another giggle escaped that I tried to suppress. "God loves me," I whispered and then giggled again.

Stella shook her head back and forth. "Of course He does. Nobody deserves it like you do."

"No." I sat up and grasped her forearms, my eyes wide with the truth. "He really loves me! And He loves you too. And everybody. It's so big. Just ask Him to show you."

"You've gone and lost your wits, Ellen. Of course God loves everybody." Stella backed away and climbed into her bed, pulling the covers over her head. "Get some sleep. We've got the auction tonight."

It struck me as I lay down, still smiling, still feeling overwhelmed with God's love for me, that Stella wasn't ready to see it yet. That I hadn't been really ready until just this moment. That God was there all along, waiting for all of us to wake up.

Thank You for waking me up, Lord.

I drifted off with a smile on my face, resting in the cradle of His arms.

$\mathcal{B}$uck stood across from Inspector Constantine in the Northwest Mounted Police headquarters in Forty Mile, trying to curb his impatience. "There has got to be something you can do."

The inspector shook his head, a frown showing underneath a thick, brown beard. "Mr. Lewis, I'm sorry about your wife, but Skagway is US territory, and besides, it sounds like an accident by your account of the story. Unfortunately these things happen."

Buck gritted his teeth and slapped his hat back on his head. "So, even if I find him and haul him back here, you won't do a thing about it, is that right?"

"I can question him, possibly send him back to Alaska, but sir, what motive would the man have to kill your wife? Would you want someone punished for an accident? It could happen to anybody."

"It didn't happen to anybody. It happened to her!" Buck's voice rose and then quieted. "It happened to me."

The inspector sighed and nodded with a compassion-ate look in his brown eyes. "Tell you what. You bring him in, and we'll get to the bottom of what happened. I will keep an eye out for him too. You say he is with one or two other fellows?"

Buck gave the descriptions of the two men he knew were traveling together again and then turned to leave. "Thank you, sir." He pushed out the door into the bright sunshine that glittered off the snow and hurt his eyes.

Tears trickled down the creases in his cheeks as he blinked rapidly. He felt like cursing but instead slapped his thigh and walked to the dogsled.

He'd been in Forty Mile for two weeks! Two weeks of almost catching up with them. But every time he got close, they moved on to another streambed or tributary of the Forty Mile River. It was as if they knew he was tracking them and were able to stay just one step ahead. But how could that be? He'd told no one his business in the little town, just presented himself as another gold seeker. It didn't make sense.

Buck led the dogs to the barely discernible street, readying them for the long mush back toward Moosehide Creek. He'd heard last night at a saloon that two men, strangers to all, were camping in an old abandoned cabin there. It was the first good lead he'd had in days. And now with Inspector Constantine's promise of support, albeit reluctant, Buck had more reason to bring them in than ever before.

Lord, I could sure use some help with this. I'm ready, Lord. Please.

The day was warmer, and Buck passed several towns-folk as he rode by on the dogsled toward the confluence in the road, one branch following the Forty Mile River west, and the other heading back toward Dawson City following the Yukon River.

Someone he recognized from the saloon last night waved as he went past and yelled, "If you're back by tomor-row, stop in for some Christmas cheer. Big celebration at the Bald Eagle!"

Everything inside Buck stopped. Tomorrow was Christmas? How could he have forgotten? Ellen's face flashed in front of him, and the letter she'd sent him burned from his coat pocket against his chest. He gripped the reins with one hand and pulled it out with the other, opening it with his teeth. It was wrinkled and creased from reading it so many times.

God, why do I feel like I've left a part of me behind? It had been different with his wife—he'd been so much older than her, strong, confident. Ellen seemed more of an equal somehow.

Buck came to the *Y* in the road and hauled on the reins. "Whoa." He looked west, toward the man who had killed his wife, and then east, toward Dawson City and Ellen. His mind made swift calculations of the time and distance. It was the middle of the day on Christmas Eve . . .

If he headed west, he would never make it back for Christmas. He'd promised Ellen. Her father had left her before Christmas. If Buck broke his promise, she would never trust him or believe him again.

But the man was so close. He could feel it. And wasn't that the reason he'd risked his life to come to this forsaken place in the middle of frozen tundra?

"Ahhhh!" He yelled with a fist toward the sky. "I just can't do it."

Chapter Thirteen

 e want Jewel! We want Jewel!"

The crowd chanted the phrase from the floor of the smoky dance hall. I stood on the stage, cowering behind the black curtain. Was I really going to do this? It wasn't too late to back out, and the good Lord must know of other ways to help the hospital than my being a wife to a miner for a day. The fact that I'd dreamed of being a bride for so long and ended up with this caused sparks of anger to flare through me.

Lord, I want my own story. Is that so wrong?

I peeked out of the crack between the curtains and scanned the large room. Kate had done a good job advertising the event as the dance hall was packed with rows of bearded, whooping miners. Additional lanterns had been brought in, and spruce boughs tied with red ribbon decorated the walls adding to the Christmas feel. I bit down on my lower lip. All of the other girls had already gone; it was my turn, or my last chance to back out.

"We want Jewel! We want Jewel!" The cheering grew louder.

One thing was clear, I couldn't stall any longer. Taking a deep breath, I parted the silky drape that served as a curtain and stepped into the bright lantern light.

The whooping miners greeted me with applause and foot stomping. There were even some Northwest Mounted Police in the back, standing out in their glossy red coats and wide, round hats that made them identifiable as the law in this place. My gaze darted from one end of the room to the other. How I wanted to turn around and run back behind that curtain! Or at least use it to cover the new green dress Kate had insisted upon, but I forced myself to stay rooted to the wooden planks of the stage.

Kate hitched up her sapphire gown and ascended the steps to stand next to me on the stage. She held up her hands and shouted above the roar. "Gentlemen, quiet, please, let us start the bidding." She motioned for me to stroll around by circling her finger. I just stared back into her excited eyes, rooted to the floor by shaking knees and a quivering stomach.

"Gentlemen! I give you the Monte Carlo's very own! The lovely Jewel of Dawson! Those of you who have danced with her know of her goodness. Gracious, half of you have proposed to her. So imagine getting your wish for a single day!"

Out of the corner of my eye, I saw her wink at the crowd.

"A wife for Christmas. Now who will start the bidding? Do I hear five hundred dollars?"

I wished for a hole to crawl in. The stomping and cheering made my heart thud too hard. I shuddered when a huge man in grimy clothes at the back of the room lifted an arm. "Five hundred," he shouted and then spit a line of tobacco juice on the shoes of his neighbor. I could make out his leering grin underneath all the beard and the glitter of lust in his eyes.

This was a terrible mistake. I couldn't go through with it. *Lord, get me out of here!*

The bidding and revelry continued to roar in my ears as the lights grew strangely dim. *Oh no, don't faint!*

"Six hundred dollars!" A stocky man with hard eyes and a mean twist to his lips yelled out.

"A thousand dollars!" Countered a newly rich, white-haired sourdough. I imagined him trying to press a kiss on me, and the urge to retch rose to the back of my throat.

"One thousand dollars. Do I hear two thousand?" Kate's eyes were truly fever pitched now.

"Five thousand." A stocky man I'd never seen before countered. *Oh no, please, God, not him.*

"Five thousand dollars!" Kate said into the quieting crowd. The other girls had brought in five to eight hundred. Five thousand dollars for a dancing girl for one day was unheard of.

I cringed at the man with the leading bid. He stared back at me and licked his lips like a cat waiting for his daily bowl of cream.

I began to pant in fear and shook my head back and forth. I looked over at Kate, pleading in my eyes.

Kate nodded her agreement that he was unacceptable and faced the crowd. "Come on, gents! I know many of you have spent more than that on an evening's worth of champagne. Jewel will make you a nice Christmas dinner and keep you company on the loneliest day of the year. Come on now. Do I hear ten thousand?"

"Twenty thousand dollars!" The man who had made the first bid raised his hand and flashed me a victorious smile. Everyone gasped at the sum, and darkness threatened the corners of my vision. Just as it was about to swallow me up, I heard a smooth male voice say into the shuffling and murmuring of the room.

"Her weight in gold."

The clamor of the room died away into turned heads and slack jaws. Kate glanced at me with her hands clasped together under her chin. "Gentlemen, did you hear that?

Her weight in gold!" Everyone's attention riveted on the tall man in black at the back of the room who had said it.

I blinked, trying to see beyond the shadows, but he wasn't even looking at me. He was busy scribbling something on a piece of paper. All I could see was the top of his smooth, black hat.

Kate cleared her throat, "Ah, sir? You do know that at sixteen dollars an ounce, your bid will come to over thirty thousand dollars?"

"Yes, I'm aware of that." He paused and finally looked up. "Have you a better offer?"

"No, no." Kate's gaze swept over the silent crowd. "Gentlemen, does anyone have a better offer?" The crowd remained silent. It was as if all the air had been belly-punched right out of them.

I felt as frozen as the outdoors. Paying that kind of money, what would he expect from me? I knew I should put a stop to this, but I couldn't seem to move. I watched, dazed, as he walked forward into the light and directed his gaze toward me for the first time.

His eyes were dark and held a glimmer of laughter in a face that was nothing short of pure masculine beauty. I'd never seen him before, but I heard Kate's sharp inhale and jerked my attention to her. "Do you know him?"

I looked back at the man as she whispered in an angry hiss, "You! I can't believe it."

He took off his hat, revealing sleek black hair, and with suppressed mirth in his eyes tipped it toward Kate. He turned back to me, locked his gaze to mine, and asked the question everyone in the room wanted answered. "How much do you weigh?"

I opened my mouth, shut it, and then opened it again.

"Ma'am, how much do you weigh?"

"I—I'm not sure, 120, I believe."

He looked me up and down, as if to judge the validity of my words. My face grew hot under his gaze, but he didn't seem to notice. He turned his attention back to his paper and scribbled some more.

Raising his head, he said to Kate, "At 120 pounds and gold at sixteen dollars an ounce, her bride's price is

$30,920." He reached into his coat and pulled out a heavy bag of gold. He held it in his hand for a moment, looking at me. "There's just one condition."

My heart dropped, and the onlookers strained forward to hear this new development.

"She has to go with me now."

"Why you no-good, black-hearted, dirty—"

"Now, Kate, you can call me names later." His deep voice was rich with humor. "Let's take care of business first, shall we? You know I won't harm the girl."

Eyes on fire, Kate motioned to the pianist to start up the clanking music and led the way to her table, pulling me along by a tight grip on my forearm.

It there ever was a time to pray, it was now.

Lord, help!

Chapter Fourteen

t was quiet and nearly empty as Kate dragged me over to her private table in the back of the barroom. She called for the scales to be brought over, her eyes slits of angry distrust toward the dark-haired man as he sat across from us.

I swallowed hard, watching them play out a scene I shouldn't be witnessing much less participating in. I took a breath, then faced the man. "Who are you?"

He bowed his head toward me and reached for my hand. His voice was all husky charm as he leaned over my hand and planted a light kiss against the back of it. "Kate, would you like to do the introductions?"

Kate gave him the dagger eyes. "I'm sure you can manage on your own. You always could."

"Very well." He gave me a knowing, wicked smile that made my hand tremble in his. "The name is Lucky and you are Jewel, yes?"

I nodded, not knowing if he should know my real name or not but thinking that like many in the Paris of the North, as Dawson was called, Lucky was another nickname.

He flashed that devastating grin as I pulled my hand from his grasp.

"Charming as ever, I see." Kate reached for the pouch of gold he'd laid on the table. "Looks like you've been lucky as usual too." She weighed the heavy bag in her hand, lifting it up and down, and eyed him with glittering distrust, then began to pour the flakes and nuggets onto the scale. She repeated the process, scale after scale, until there were little but a few grains of sparkling dust left in the bag. She flung it across the table at him.

"Why her? Why spend all this money for a day with one of my girls? Are you trying to make some kind of point?"

I turned, wanting to slink away and disappear. These two had something to work out between them, and I knew better than to be in the middle of it.

"Kate. I realize you think you can't trust me, but I had my reasons, and a deal is a deal." He leaned across the table and touched her cheek.

A look flashed across her eyes I'd never seen before. Kate was always so dispassionate, so in control, but in that moment I saw hurt and longing and love.

Kate loved this man.

"I can't do it." The words I'd been holding in all night tumbled out.

Kate swung toward me with raised brows and compressed lips. "Of course you can. We made an agreement, and you will stick by it. The hospital, remember?"

I turned toward Lucky who shrugged at me in understanding.

"Now." Kate clapped her hands together to gain both our attention. "Jewel will leave with you tonight, but you listen to me and listen good. She is to be treated like a lady the entire time." She eyed Lucky and smacked her palm down on the table. "I'd ask for your word on that, but we both know how well you keep promises. Just know, if she comes back damaged goods, I'll hunt you down myself, and what I have imagined doing to you this last year—"

The man's jaw clenched, and I got the distinct impression Kate was getting through his glib exterior. "I'm flattered, Kate. I didn't know you still cared so much."

Kate reddened and sputtered as it finally dawned on me who this man was. Lucky was her long-lost fiancé. So, what in heaven's name did he want with me?

"Go!" She pointed her finger toward the door. "Just go."

Minutes later and garbed in my winter gear, I followed Lucky's long stride through the front door. The cold reminded me of the stark realities of this place, how precarious life was, how I didn't know what was to happen next. It was as if I was stepping into the great unknown, a frozen future that held the possibilities of a dream city.

Lucky stopped at the edge of the raised walkway and flung out an arm. "Your chariot awaits, ma'am."

I stared at the conveyance and gasped. It was a pretty, little, white-painted wooden sleigh with gleaming steel runners, hitched to a beautiful team of huskies. I looked up into his dark, laughing eyes. "Where are we going?"

"That, my dear, is a surprise. May I help you in?"

We walked to the edge of the sleigh where I accepted Lucky's offered hand and climbed inside, settling onto a deep, cushioned bench lined with fur robes. Lucky took another fur robe and, to my further astonishment, tucked it over and around my shoulders, covering me in its silky depths. "Warm enough?"

I nodded, a little laugh escaping me. This man was the epitome of surprise.

Lucky climbed in beside me and grasped the reins. He took a moment to light a cigar, clamped it between his teeth, and grinned around it. "Hold on tight; we have time to make."

His deep chuckle and the smell of the cigar drifted over to me as he commanded the dogs and started us with a jolt. The buildings flashed by as we fairly flew down the street.

The snow was hard packed and glistening in the moonlight. We were soon out of town and following a trail that ran along the river. My breath came in excited puffs around my face, but I wasn't cold. I was never so warm and trembling with excitement.

"You and Kate know each other well?" I glanced over to him.

He looked at me, black brows furrowed together, and then directed his attention back to the dogs. "You could say that."

"She still loves you, you know. I saw it in her eyes." I was taking the risk of angering him in saying that, but I had to know what had gone wrong.

"Hate is more likely the word you're looking for. That's what I saw in her eyes."

"Haven't you ever heard that there is a fine line between love and hate? And anyway, think how this looks.

Bidding on me for a wife? It must be tearing her apart. Why did you do it?"

"Do what? Bid on you? Or run out and leave her at the altar?" His voice was filled with self-loathing.

"Both, I guess."

"You'll find out soon enough why I won you. The other? I just couldn't go through with it."

I paused, the anxiety of his answer about winning me scattered my thoughts like buckshot through my mind. I took a determined breath. "Didn't you love her? Didn't you want to make her your wife?"

The moon cast a silver glow against his profile. His jaw hardened and his eyes narrowed. "I loved her, still do. There isn't a day that goes by that I don't think of her and miss her. But the good Lord knows what I think of marriage."

"What do you think of marriage?" I pulled the fur closer around my neck where the wind was whistling in.

"I think it's a waste of paper. It doesn't mean anything. People do what they want to do with or without it."

"Why do you think that?"

Lucky's gaze slid to mine as he let out a bark of laughter. "You some kind of head doctor?"

"No, I just . . . well, I think I might be able to understand. My family was . . . broken."

He chewed on the cigar stub a bit. "I don't know why I'm telling you this. I've never told anyone, but my father, he wasn't much of a husband and broke my mother's heart over and over with other women."

"Were you afraid Kate would do that to you?"

"Maybe. Or I'd do it to her. There's a thousand ways to back out of those marriage vows. In good times and bad, in sickness and health—"

"I know." I gripped my hands together under the warm fur. "My mother was sick. Not physically all of the time, but"—I patted my chest—"in here. My father didn't know what to do with her, I guess. He left us when I was a young child. I took care of her and my brother." I touched Lucky's taut arm wielding the reins. "Everyone fails at some time or another, but I still hope to get married someday."

Lucky turned to me, the reins going slack in his hands, the dogs running as if they loved it, as if they could run so swift and sure all night, all on their own. "How can you? Aren't you afraid the man you marry will leave you like your father did?"

"Yes, I'm afraid. But I'm more afraid of living without him. I have to give him a chance. I have to give us a chance. I might fail him too. I think I will in little everyday ways, but I will open my heart to him as if I had the perfect childhood. That's a choice, you know. Everyone deserves a chance, don't you think?" I closed my eyes and saw the *him* in my statements. I saw Buck.

Lucky was quiet for a long moment. "You really think she still loves me?"

I laughed and clasped my hands together under the fur. "Oh yes, I am quite sure. She's still mad at you and scared too, but I think if you go to her and tell her the truth, what you've told me . . . she will forgive you."

Lucky faced forward and flicked the reins to make the dogs go faster. He didn't say another word.

We raced along through the thick forest, up steep hills, and speeding down shallow valleys to the sound of the jingling bells on the dogs' harnesses. It was nearing midnight. Almost Christmas day.

All of a sudden a light appeared before us. As we neared it, the light became a window. It was a cabin, all the windows glowing with warm yellow light and smoke coming from the chimney.

"Is that your cabin?" I asked above the wailing wind.

"No, ma'am. It belongs to a friend."

"A friend?" Should I be afraid?

Lucky just chuckled and hauled back on the reins. The dogs slowed to a gliding stop. "Don't worry. It's someone I've known for years."

I stared at the yellow-hewed log cabin in awe. Two stories high and blazing with light that turned the snow around the cabin into a million scattered, sparkling diamonds. A giant spruce wreath with a big red ribbon hung on the front door, and the yard had a neat, shoveled path. It was as if a painting had come to life.

Lucky jumped down and came around to my side. He reached for my hand and helped me out of the sleigh. I wanted to ask questions, but I couldn't seem to speak. I was too busy soaking up the beauty of the scene.

Lucky tucked my arm in his and led me to the front door. It opened before we reached it. A tremor of nervous expectation made my knees wobble as I entered the room where a cheery fire crackled in the hearth. A giant Christmas tree, smelling of fresh-cut pine, glowing with candles and decorated with pinecones and holly garland, stood in one corner of the room.

The door shut behind me and I spun around.

A man stepped forward, coming out of the shadows. My hand rose to my mouth as tears, immediate and drowning my vision, sprang to my eyes. "Buck?"

"I promised we'd be together for Christmas, didn't I?"

He appeared tired but happy, as if he'd fought a battle and won. I looked from his dear face to Lucky's grinning one and then back again.

"I told you I'd make it before midnight." Lucky's voice broke through the silence.

Buck gave Lucky's shoulder a solid thump that turned into a sideways hug. "I knew I could count on you. You have my thanks."

I stood still and trembling—my knees, my stomach, my chin, all trembling. "You planned this? You had Lucky bid for me?"

Buck took the steps that separated us and drew me into his arms. He didn't say anything for a long moment, just leaned his face onto the top of my head and held me tight. His breath moved in and out of my hair. His love wrapped around my body—a warm, tender wave of promises kept.

"But how?" I whispered, looking up into his face.

Buck straightened. His crystal blue eyes stared deep into my brown ones. His thumb came up to caress my cheek. "I knew I couldn't get to Dawson in time for Christmas so I sent a telegram to my cousin here and asked for a favor."

"Lucky is your cousin?"

Buck chuckled. "Lucky is Stephen's nickname since coming to Alaska. After I got married and settled down, he got itchy feet and traveled around the state. Picked up a love for card games and the name. I'd heard he was staying near Fort Reliance, which is only eight miles from Dawson, so I telegrammed the fort and someone got him the message. He telegrammed back about the auction. Said everyone for miles was going to attend. The thought of you being some other man's wife, even for a day, made me"—he grasped the sides of my face—"feel sick. I was ready to race to Dawson, try to make it in time, but then Lucky had an idea. He knew about this cabin and thought it would be fun to surprise you."

My gaze shot to Lucky. "You have to tell Kate. What she must be imagining right now."

Lucky nodded at Buck and placed his hat back on his head. "I see why they call her the Jewel of Dawson. I'll be heading back to town. I'm thinking I'd like to have a wife for Christmas too."

"It's about time." Buck laughed. "Godspeed, my friend."

Lucky leaned down, took my hand, and kissed the back of it with elegant flair. He peered up at me over my hand and said in a low voice, "Thank you, ma'am. Your courage has an inspired effect."

I squeezed his hand tight. "Kate has courage enough for the both of you, I think. Trust her."

After Lucky left, Buck took me back into his arms. "I love you, Ellen."

I hadn't expected to hear it yet. I held on to his shoulders and wanted to say the words back, but first I had to know. "What about your wife? Did you find the man who shot her?" *How are you, really? Are you ready to love me with your whole heart?*

Buck led me over to the sofa that faced the fire. He sat beside me and took my hands in his strong, warm ones. "I couldn't find them. I came close many times, but they were never . . . predictable. A few hours ago I got word that two strangers were camping on Moosehide Creek. I stocked up on provisions and readied my dog team. I was going to go, I was determined to go, but I knew if I did I would never make it to this cabin in time. I was standing there with my team all ready at the *Y* in the road. Losing my wife was the—" He stopped, his throat working with the emotion, tears shining in his eyes.

I squeezed his hand. He leaned forward and placed his head against my head. "It was the hardest thing I've ever experienced. But I couldn't let you go. I knew if I chose to go after them, I would never have you." He turned his face into my neck. "I had to let her go."

"Oh, Buck." We cried together for Deborah, Kalage, his Little Two-Face. My tears dripped into his hair as we cried for a lost life, a lost wife.

After many moments I pulled back. "You'll always love her, Buck. It's okay. You have enough heart, I think, for both of us."

He stared deep into my eyes, his big, warm, strong hands a butterfly's touch against my face. "How did I get so blessed to find you?"

"No." I touched his face as he did mine. "I'm the blessed one. God has given me the desire of my heart—my own story with you. How did I get a second chance at life? How did God lead me to you?"

The clock started to chime the midnight hour. "It's Christmas," I said as we pulled back. Candlelight flickered across Buck's rugged face making me take a sudden breath at the beauty of his damp eyelashes.

Words came to me. "'For unto us a child is born, unto us a son is given: and the government shall be upon his shoulder: and his name shall be called Wonderful, Counselor, The mighty God, The everlasting Father, The Prince of Peace.'"

A smile lit Buck's eyes. He began to sing in a soft, rich baritone:

> O come, O come, Emmanuel,
> And ransom captive Israel,
> That mourns in lonely exile here,
> Until the Son of God appear.
> Rejoice! Rejoice! Emmanuel
> Shall come to thee, O Israel!

I joined my voice with his for the second verse of the Christmas song:

O come, Thou Rod of Jesse, free,

Thine own from Satan's tyranny,

From depths of Hell Thy people save,

And give them victory o'er the grave.

Rejoice! Rejoice! Emmanuel

Shall come to thee, O Israel!

"Shall come to thee, O Israel." It was perfect. God had ransomed me from my captivity. I was no longer in lonely exile. He had set my feet upon the firm foundation of His great love and then given me a story of my own.

"I didn't know you could sing like that." I touched Buck's solemn face and felt the day-old whiskers underneath my fingertips, marveling that God knows the number of hairs on our heads. "You have a wonderful voice, Buck."

"I guess there's a lot we don't know about each other, but I think—"

"Yes?" My heart started drumming in my chest.

"I was thinking that—" He paused. He was nervous, after everything we had been through together, he was still unsure. "I won you for a wife for Christmas day, but—" He looked down at our clasped hands. "I was wondering . . ."

"Yes?"

". . . if you would like to be my wife for the rest of our days." He looked up from my hand and met my gaze. His eyes, so light blue as to appear glowing, burned with what seemed like hope as he asked the question.

A half laugh/half sob escaped my throat as I pressed my hand against my heart. I'd never thought to have anyone of my own. I'd never thought to be free enough or lucky enough to find love. Yet here it was in the form of a man I hadn't been able to imagine until I met him. God had known all along His plans for my future. I breathed out that one word with everything in me.

"Yes."

Buck leaned forward and swept me into his arms.

"I love you, Buck," I whispered as I tilted my head back to stare into his eyes.

My breath caught as he seemed to study every feature of my face, stopping at my lips. He leaned toward me, and when I thought he would kiss me, he stopped just short and said, "Take a breath, Ellen, before you pass out."

I bit my bottom lip and smiled up into his eyes, those ice blue crystals that were warm now, that I would get to gaze into for the rest of my days. "I thought you were going to kiss me."

He caressed my cheek with his thumb. "Just taking my time."

His words sent a warm wave through my body. Of course. We had the rest of our lives together. Then he crushed his lips to mine with gentle demand.

Every icicle around my heart melted into a pool of ecstasy . . . and I floated.

I floated like the snowflake, a delicate, intricate, one-of-a-kind, God-crafted snowflake that never melts, that was made for eternity. Together we were strong and glittering and eternally glorious.

Rejoice! Rejoice, Emmanuel. My heart sang the song.

I was *His* and *his* and *mine.* I was whole.

Floating . . . eternal . . . in an everlasting pool of love.

Dear Reader,

Have you ever considered the snowflake? I have. I have
a fascination with them. They say snowflakes are one of
a kind, like fingerprints. Can you imagine how many
snowflakes are in a handful of snow? A yard full? A city's
worth? And that's just in one snowfall. What about a winter's worth of snowflakes across the entire world? What
about every snowflake that has or will ever fall? Can you
imagine the diversity in each intricate design? The perfectly symmetrical arms that appear like sparkling glass
under a microscope? The bends and twists, the nubs and
branches on a piece of floating, fluffy frozen water? Only
God has that much imagination, that much creativity, that

much timeless knowledge and wisdom. Only God could build a snowflake with each one having its own identity.

We are like the snowflake. Fantastic and unfathomable and fragile. Our lives are a moment in time, but that moment is all ours. No one like you was ever made or ever to be made. If God took the effort to make each snowflake with its own unique shape, how much more did He expend on you, His beloved, in His image?

We forget, I think, how valuable we are to Him. When the snowflake melts, what does it become? Streams and rivers, lakes and oceans. Life-giving water. God created one-of-a-kind water droplets for you to drink. I can't fathom such love.

Dear beloved reader, do not sell yourself short. Do not think for a moment that you don't mean everything to Him. Do not let man and Satan, sin and evil, rob you of your worth. After all, God gave His one and only Son for you.

Remember that the next time you look in the mirror and see only shortcomings and failures. Remember. It's hard, I know. But I promise, I will try and remember it too.

If you would like to learn more about the science of snowflakes, here is a wonderful Web site: www.its.caltech.edu/~atomic/snowcrystals/class/class.htm.

Learn more about Jamie Carie's books at www.jamie carie.com.

Discussion Questions

1. Ellen's brother, Jonah, suffered with mental illness triggered when their father walked out on them. Describe a situation when you or someone you know struggled with emotional or mental difficulties (i.e., depression, anxiety disorders, obsessive-compulsive disorder, abandonment issues, bipolar disorder, post-traumatic stress disorder, etc.)? What sort of treatment did you/they turn to?

2. What role should the body of Christ play in reaching out to people who struggle with mental illness and/or emotional trauma?

3. The characters on board the ice-locked steamship are forced to make a decision—sit out the winter on the ship or risk a harrowing trek across Alaska to reach Dawson City. Which group would you be in? What personality type are you? (Risk taker? Thrill seeker? Overly cautious? Conservative?)

4. When, if ever, have you had to make a big decision, and though you prayed, you didn't receive a definitive answer from the Lord? What did you do? What do these Scripture verses mean to you in regards to making big decisions?

"Answer me when I call to you, O my righteous God. Give me relief from my distress; be merciful to me and hear my prayer" (Ps. 4:1 NIV).

"Hear my prayer, O LORD, listen to my cry for help; be not deaf to my weeping. For I dwell with you as an alien, a stranger, as all my fathers were" (Ps. 39:12 NIV).

"Thy Word is a lamp unto my feet, and a light unto my path" (Ps. 119:105 KJV).

5. Buck is the kind of man folklore is made from. What is it about the strong, confident, "leader of men" type that is so attractive? If married, what type of man did you choose and why? If single, which type of man are you attracted to and why do you think that is?

6. On the trail Sinclair is accused of stealing food. Describe a time when you were falsely accused of something or falsely accused someone else. Read and discuss Mark 15 when Jesus is accused and crucified.

7. What do you think of Kate? How would you react if you were offered help by a prostitute or someone of ill repute?

8. When Buck leaves Dawson, Ellen struggles with loneliness and longing for him. Everyone feels lonely at times. What triggers this for you? How do you cope?

9. The holiday season can be tough for some people. What are the best aspects of Christmas? The worst?

10. What does the Bible say about loneliness? Jesus endured much suffering during His crucifixion, but it was not until He could no longer feel His Father's presence that He finally broke and called out in desperation, *"Eloi, Eloi, lama sabachthani?"*—which means, "My God, my God, why have you forsaken me?" (Mark 15:34 NIV). Why do you think God designed us to need one another and His presence in our lives?

11. Describe a time when you didn't feel God's presence in your life. What led up to it, and how did you get it back?

12. The reader never finds out what happens when Lucky leaves to beg Kate to take him back. Do you like loose ends in a story, or would you rather the author neatly tie everything up before the end? Explain.

13. Buck is forced to make a decision between holding on to his deceased wife or embracing a new life with Ellen. What are your experiences with death, and how have you coped?

14. All of my books end "happily ever after." What do you think "happily ever after" looks like on earth? In heaven?